SHOWDOWN

Con James appeared from behind the far side of the building. He was flanked by Mac Cobb, Jasey Crook, and a man Cord recalled from the soddy because he had only one front tooth, and that one gold.

Everyone held guns, but Cord knew with hollow certainty he had lost the moment. He should have blasted them soon as they came into sight.

"Throw 'em down," Con James ordered, watching close through his owly eyes.

Disarmed, they were dead. Cord knew that sure as sunup.

"I said throw 'em down." James grinned. "It is over for you."

Cord shot the outlaw with the gold tooth.

Chi was on her stomach in the street, her Colt extended. She popped off a covering shot. James was lining on her when Cord brought up the rifle.

CORD
Gunman Winter

Owen Rountree

BALLANTINE BOOKS • NEW YORK

Library of Congress Catalog Card Number: 82-90938

ISBN 0-345-29591-9

Manufactured in the United States of America

First Edition: July 1983

Chapter One

THE CANTINA WAS CALLED *LOS TRES Hermanos*, although the *cantinera* was a plump cheerful woman with a wide dark smile, a mustache, and no brothers at all. It was one of several small mysteries Cord was enjoying. The way into the *Hermanos* was through an unmarked doorway off an alley filled with garbage and barnyard livestock and manure. The cantina room was a dim fortress of windowless adobe, its air thick with the stench from the alleyway.

But when you passed through and climbed four steps, you came out into sunlight on the patio, and it was here that Cord and Chi had gotten used to doing their drinking since coming into Ciudad Juárez two weeks earlier. The patio was a little above street level and surrounded by a waist-high 'dobe wall. At each corner a poinsettia bloomed in a clay pot. The four round tables of unfinished wood were bleached nearly white by the sunlight; a dozen or so chairs were divided among them. The patio faced out onto the town plaza, and Cord and Chi sat at the table nearest the wall, where they could watch the *ciudadanos* go about their business beneath the bright thin winter sun.

"There are times," Cord said, "when this country reminds me of the Staked Plains. This time of year, mainly, when the light shines low and glary, and the horizon country is flat against the sky and a long ways off at the same time. I remember some days . . ." Cord chuckled to himself, and Chi raised her eyebrows and studied him. But Cord just chuckled again and sipped at his glass. They were drinking from tall mugs of dark beer with thick caramelly heads that never seemed to go flat. Each of them had a salt shaker, and between them on a plate were a dozen wedges of fresh lemon.

"We were north of Lubbock somewheres," Cord said. "Up near to the Prairie Dog Town Fork of the Red River."

"Who was?"

"There's this story I'm going to tell you."

"Ah," Chi said with saintly patience. She was having a good time.

Across the street was the *Plaza Mayor*, and in its middle there was a crèche, a little half-shed of weathered planks; inside were carvings from juniper of the Virgin Mother, Joseph, and the Three Kings. The statues had been freshly painted in exquisite detail, though they were probably ancient as the town. A papier-mâché bundle swathed in white linen lay on a bed of straw in a manger, and straw was strewn around the beat-dirt floor. A post-and-pole fence enclosed the display, and within were live animals: goats, kids, lambkins, a splay-legged colt. Half a dozen dark-skinned children were hanging on the fence, laughing and squealing and reaching between the rails to grab and pet the baby animals, which could not have been much different from the animals they had lived around all their lives. Except these were touched by the magic of Christmas, which had been the day before.

"I was a kid," Cord said, "my second year away from home and still thinking that tending cows on the open range was the finest life a man could ever wish—and it was, compared to what I'd left behind in East Texas." Cord shook his head and muttered something.

"How's that?" Chi asked.

"Jim," Cord repeated. "I was thinking of my brother Jim back on that hardscrabble ranch where we were kids together. You remember Jim."

Sure, he thought, *she remembered Jim.*

"Mmmm," Chi said by way of neutral encouragement.

"Anyway," Cord said, brightening again, "this outfit— the one I was working for then—it was owned by an hombre named Hacksaw Harris, and it was spring and time for branding. Bert Golden was the foreman, and we'd set up camp near to a little headwaters creek and started gathering off the desert, which is what it was most of the year in those parts."

On the other side of the street a man and woman passed, both dressed all in white, the man in a loose-fitting white blouse, white trousers, and a dashing white sash, the woman in a full-skirted white dress with a deep, square-cut bodice. Cord thought the woman looked strikingly like Chi: high cheekbones, glittering dark eyes, the same challenging smile animating her olive features. She wore her hair like Chi too, long dark braids to below her waist, tied off with rawhide thongs trimmed with turquoise. But Chi would never dress like the woman; at least Cord had never seen her any other way than she was now, in dark leather britches tucked into the uppers of knee-high tooled boots, a black flat-brimmed sombrero, and a wool serape that served her in any weather.

Cord looked at his partner, tried for a moment to picture her dressed in swirling white skirts and a tight low bodice. Chi watched him with her faint knowing grin, and Cord, momentarily disconcerted, let go his imagining and picked up his story.

"That year there was a greenhorn who had signed on for the branding, a heavyset older fellow named George Straight. This George had come west from working as a prison guard at Sing Sing, in New York State. He told us it had come to him one day that he could not stomach any more of the pen, that he had to have nothing but wide open spaces for the rest of his life. Well, he got that all right, out on the *Llano Estacado.* You got to admire him for working out his change like that, except maybe for the one thing, which was horses. George had too much gut and not enough leg to sit a horse properly, and he didn't like animals much to start with. Jesus!" Cord shook his head and chuckled some more.

"Anyway," he went on, "we'd been branding in open country, and George was packing the irons when we came to one of those alkali sinks. The cattle had churned the whole thing to the color of a gravestone and not much thicker, but it was the only water for your horse in miles.

"But old George's sorrel mare would not lower her head to drink."

The plump *cantinera* came out and sat fresh glasses of dark beer before them. Chi murmured, "*Gracias, señora.*"

"You got to see it," Cord said with great glee. "Here is George Straight, out in about a foot and a half of mud and six inches of dirty water, and his mare gone contrary in front of everyone. George tries pushing down on the mare's head, and he tries cursing. Nothing works. So he pulls one of those irons out of the old scabbard he is carrying them in, and he brings it down dead square between the sorrel's ears.

"Maybe he figures that will teach her some sense," Cord said. "What it does is knock her out cold as a wedge. Down she goes like she is shot, *kerflop,* into the mud and water, legs splayed out like a trophy rug. George goes down with her, and before he can kick free she comes around and starts kicking and rolling, covering herself and this greenhorn with mud thick as plaster.

"The rest of us," Cord said, "sat there horseback, watching George and his foolishness, and shooting looks at Bert Golden, wondering how he is going to handle this. Finally George gets his boots undone from the stirrups, and the mare lurches to her feet, leaving George on his hands and knees in the mud, breathing hard. Bert Golden is studying him like he is a new species of critter.

"Finally George Straight looks up at him.

"'Well, George,' Bert says, 'you catch up.' And the rest of us turn and ride on. It was near dark before George came along, the mud all over him and the sorrel dried hard as slate and the same color. From that day on we called him the Spook." Cord looked at Chi to gauge how amused she was by this tale. She was staring back stony-eyed.

"*Madre Dios,*" she said. "This is what I get for a partner." But then she had to look away, unable to keep from laughing. "Here's to spooks," she said. "To all the spooks and *brujos* and witches we ever knew." They touched glasses and drank.

From where they sat the Rio Grande was a couple of hundred yards away, and across it the outskirts of El Paso, the farthest west Texas outpost. But in the Mexican plaza on this holiday afternoon Cord was the only gringo. He sprinkled coarse-ground salt on the back of his hand, licked it off, and bit the pulp from a wedge of lemon, then chased the sour-salt flavor with a deep swig of the heavy beer. The couple in white were on a bench across the plaza, their heads together. The man said something and the woman laughed gaily, the clear pure tones of her pleasure stippling the quiet afternoon. Cord felt the sun's warmth on his hands and face, and he was glad of Chi's companionship.

The morning before they had lingered over coffee after a

long late breakfast. Chi surprised Cord by reaching under her serape and setting a small sandalwood box on the table before him. Inside, cushioned on a scrap of velvet, rested a Hamilton pocket watch in a gold case. Cord snapped it open and read the inscription engraved on the inside of the cover, written in Spanish over Chi's name.

"*Feliz Navidad,*" Chi said softly.

His gift to her was wrapped in a chamois cloth, and when she undid it her eyes quickened and then softened. Cord had visited a metalsmith earlier that week. The artisan had fashioned a silver bracelet, wide yet thin as the soft metal would allow, set with matched pieces of turquoise.

Chi's fingers toyed with it now as they sat on the cantina's patio. Cord had been almost afraid to present it to her, but the watch made it all right. In the ten years they had ridden together they had never exchanged Christmas gifts, but Cord sensed their life was changing in lots of ways. The partnering was working better than ever, and breaks were falling their way. At least the fears and dangers and doubts had been minor and manageable.

Cord thought of saying these things, which was invariably hard. The bracelet would serve. Chi understood. She gave him the gold watch.

Explanations were not their way, because talk never solved anything and sure as hell never lasted. Still . . . Cord reached across the table for Chi's hand.

"Listen," he began.

From the doorway the *cantinera* called out into the cantina's dimness. Chi said, "*Sí,*" and because she had not moved her hand or gaze from him, Cord did not know to whom she was responding.

But then the *cantinera* hoisted her bulk up the four steps and came to the table, and the moment was broken. Her Spanish was too rapid-fire for Cord to follow.

"*Sí,*" Chi said again. "*Por favor.*" To Cord she said, "There's a man who wants to talk to us."

"Gringo?"

"Yes."

Yes. Well, that changed everything for the time being. Men were too often looking to talk to them, him and Chi. There was money on their heads, having to do primarily with banks and gunwork, and from time to time they were the objects of the law's unsolicited interest. Besides, over the years Cord had gained considerable repute as a man with gunhand speed and steadiness. Mindless as it was, that alone was reason enough for some men to try killing him, men who operated out of the twisted notion that such repute was a fine thing to seek out and own. Living with all that was part of the deal Cord and Chi had worked out in choosing to live in the West by their own rules, but sometimes—now was one—it meant putting future plans aside in favor of present survival.

The man who came up the steps in the sunshine was in his early to middle twenties, maybe ten years younger than Cord. He was rangy, with long legs that looked longer in stovepipe gabardine trail pants. Around his narrow waist was a gunbelt, in its holster a Smith and Wesson Schofield .45. He had straight, not-too-broad shoulders, and the sleeves of his woolen shirt were rolled up and the top buttons undone, as if even the mild warmth of the Mexican winter was too much for him. He wore a palomino Stetson with a rolled brim. His hair was dark and needed cutting, and though he had made some effort at brushing off the dust of whatever road he'd come riding down, his boots were scuffed and turning down at the heels.

The man stood at the top step and took in Cord and Chi, then the rest of the patio and the plaza beyond, like a stage actor counting the house.

He came across, stood over the table, and said to Cord, "You're not wearing a weapon."

"Nice day out here," Cord said. "I didn't figure I'd need one, not to drink a beer in the sunshine. Could be I was wrong."

The man gave that some thought.

"Now, my partner here," Cord said, "I don't know if she's wearing a gun or not, because as a general rule she straps it on under that serape, about where her hands are hiding. I've never known her *not* to wear a gun, but there's always a first time." He looked at Chi. "You never can tell about women."

But Chi was watching the man with something like amusement. That eased Cord's mind. Chi had instincts about people that turned out right most of the time. Besides, the man did not have the pure nostril-pinching smell of trouble. There would be no shoot-'em-up nonsense to break the spell of *this* afternoon.

"Can I sit down?" the man said.

"Sit, *muchacho*," Chi said with grave politeness. If the man realized the diminutive was a tease, he did not show it.

"That dark beer—" the man said. "Is that all they got?"

"Do you want one?" Chi said.

The man shrugged. Chi called in Spanish, and the three of them waited in silence until the *cantinera* brought another glass.

The man sipped, made a thoughtful face, and said, "My name is Thomas Bowen."

"*Hola*, Thomas Bowen," Chi said. She looked at Cord. "Do we know any Thomas Bowens?" All this came sober as prayer, but Chi was having a high time with the young man. Maybe she was too long with just his company, Cord thought.

"What do you want with us, Thomas Bowen?" Chi asked.

"I am deputy sheriff of Prine County, Kansas," Bowen announced, as if that explained everything.

Cord sighed. He had no use for lawmen. He'd seen his share in his years on the outlaw trail, had even spent a few months in their jails. They were not bad people, except they would never leave you be.

"You are a ways from Kansas, Deputy Sheriff," Cord said.

"There's a reason. You got the makings?"

He was better than Cord at rolling smokes, but then, most everyone was. When he was finished, Chi took the pouch and rolled two more, passing one to Cord.

"The seat of Prine County is a town named Weed," Bowen said. "I rode out from there six weeks back, ten days before Thanksgiving. I have been through three states and two territories, following up everything from gossip to rumor to for-sure eyewitness swear-to-God fact." Bowen blew out smoke. "I was looking for a man."

"This man got a name?"

"Yeah," Bowen said. "But I haven't come to that part yet. What I want with this man isn't official lawman business, even though it was my boss the sheriff asked me to go on the search. I was doing a favor, not following an order."

"Who's sheriff up in Prine County these days?" Chi asked. "I haven't been up that way for years."

"Miss," Bowen said, "you have never been up there. If you had, they would still be talking about you."

Chi smiled at the compliment, and once again, even in the middle of this roundabout story, Cord thought how good it was to see her relaxed and happy with herself and him.

"All right," Chi said, "but who is sheriff?"

"John P. Kinsolving."

Cord drank half the beer in his glass, then drew in

cigarette smoke and let it dribble out in a thin stream. Kinsolving was a name he knew.

"What does he want with me?"

"I don't know." Bowen was playing straight, now that Cord had owned up to himself. "All he told me was find you and fetch you back—if you'd come. I know it doesn't have anything to do with you busting banks here and there. He doesn't mean to take you in or anything."

Bowen finished his beer. "I didn't ask for this. I didn't know how you'd take this, but I'm not looking for any gun trouble. Maybe I came on a little strong. You know how it is."

The deputy pushed back his chair. "That's all of it. What happens next is up to you." But at the top of the four steps he turned. "I was to ask, that's all. I wasn't supposed to try to talk you into anything."

"Is that what Kinsolving told you?"

"'You ask,' he said. 'And you only do it once.' Those were his words."

Chi was watching Cord expectantly, and Cord looked past her to the plaza and the laughing children and the animals, and the river and the border station on the bridge, staring hard like the scene was a stagedrop curtain about to part and reveal the deep past.

"Yeah," Cord said. "I can hear his voice."

Chapter Two

THE MAN NAMED JASPERSON DID NOT LOOK like a banker. Most bankers Cord had encountered wore long faces and dark clothing, like there was something mournful about spending your working days surrounded by other people's money. Jasperson wore a cream-colored suit and a linen shirt with a four-in-hand tie. He held a flat-brimmed fawn Stetson in both hands. On the better side of forty, he had a round open face and manicured fingernails, and he projected serenity.

Cord and Chi were passing time in Flagstaff, Arizona. It was November, six weeks before their encounter with Deputy Sheriff Thomas Bowen on the patio of *Los Tres Hermanos*. They had narrowed the possibilities down to moving south toward the desert country or west to the coast, but then banker Jasperson knocked on the door of Chi's room at the Holme House Hotel. When Cord opened it, standing well to the side, Jasperson gestured meaninglessly with the fawn Stetson and said, "May I come in?"

"Why?"

Jasperson looked up and down the hotel corridor. "I'm a banker and you are a bank robber. We might kick that around a little."

Cord glanced over his shoulder. Chi was frowning. She liked people better when it was clear what they were about.

While Cord was looking to her, Jasperson slipped into the room, pulling the door shut behind him.

"You take some awful chances, mister," Chi said.

"I know," Jasperson said. "Right there is the root of my trouble." He looked around again, then sat in a straight-backed chair next to the room's only window. Chi was on the bed, her legs tucked under her. Cord put his back against the wall next to the door.

"The first chance I took," Jasperson said, "was getting married. I married a woman named Victoriana Carpenter." He said it like the name meant something. To Cord it did not. "Truth to tell, Victoriana is not an attractive woman. In fact, you would not wish to take her to a dog show, out of fear she might win a ribbon. But at the time I married her, she was the only heir of Senator Robert Carpenter. And sure enough, the senator met his maker within six months."

"There was a break," Cord said.

"Yes," Jasperson said, "and no. Victoriana inherited the old orator's not inconsiderable loot, and by a combination of cajolery and threat, perhaps some light lying, I got it away from her. I made some investments, so to speak. A silver mine in New Mexico, a kerosene well in Pennsylvania, a wheat farm in south Texas."

"There's no way you can grow wheat in south Texas," Cord said.

"I know that," Jasperson said, with a trace of irritation. "At least I do now." He took a packet of factory-made cigarillos from his inside coat pocket and passed it around. Chi took two and tucked them under the band of her sombrero.

"In a relatively brief period," Jasperson said, "the money was mostly gone. Victoriana was more homely than ever, and had gained weight as well. She has red hair. In her natural state in the privacy of our bedroom, she looks like a carrot stuck in a lump of suet.

"I used the last of the senator's money to buy a bank in Las Vegas, Nevada, named the Second Guarantee Trust, and a mistress named Pamela. Now, this will surprise you: The bank did reasonably well, and Pamela has not yet tried to blackmail me."

"You're on a hot streak." Cord wondered where this was leading, and why he was listening.

"Yes indeed. But then there was all that money around all the time. Pamela likes pretty things and I like investing. It's at the point right now where I don't have to worry much about figuring out ways to avoid Victoriana's carnal demands, because any day someone is going to discover how much money I've embezzled from my own bank, and when that happens they will send me to prison for a very long time."

"Get to it," Chi said.

"I want you to rob my bank." Jasperson smiled broadly and turned both palms out, as if delivering a benediction.

The Second Guarantee Trust of Las Vegas, Jasperson told Cord and Chi in that Flagstaff hotel room, was a depository for Federal Reserve funds, in the form of new cash from the Denver Mint on its way to Los Angeles. In one week's time, a shipment of $10,000 would spend a night in Jasperson's vault, awaiting the arrival of a Los Angeles Federal Marshal to accompany it the rest of the way. This was the money Jasperson wanted Cord and Chi to steal.

"Here is what you will do," Jasperson said. "One week from today, on the twenty-seventh, you will ride into Las Vegas at four in the afternoon. You will knock on the locked front door of the bank, and when I come to answer you will draw down on me. I will unlock the door. The bank will have been closed for an hour by then.

"Inside with me will be Mrs. Peet, my bookkeeper, and Mister Chinske, my head cashier. You will tell them to lie facedown on the floor. They will do it, believe me. Mrs. Peet will whimper, and Mister Chinske will wet himself, or worse.

"You will take the ten thousand dollars and ride out. About five miles from town there is a safe place where you will leave one third of the money for me. That will be enough to bring my books out of fiction and back to a semblance of fact."

Jasperson dropped the butt of his cigarillo to the floor and ground it out with the heel of his shoe. "Do we have a deal?" he asked, staring down at the crushed butt. He looked up expectantly. "Of course we do."

"No, we do not," Cord said. "Anyway, not the way you've got it figured."

"After dark, for starters," Chi said. "When the place is empty."

Jasperson shook his head. "There must be witnesses. Otherwise it will not look right for me."

"There are other ways," Chi said to Cord. "How about if he is in there alone and we shoot him up a little? That would make it look right for him." She smiled at Jasperson. "We won't do you much permanent harm."

"I don't think I like that idea," Jasperson said.

"The trouble is," Cord said patiently, "witnesses make it rough on us. All they have to say is something about an Anglo man and a Mexican woman and the law gets a fair notion of who they are talking about. All of a sudden we are real famous in southern Nevada. Got our picture up everywhere."

"You come in first," Jasperson said. "She stays back. You get them down on the floor and you do all the talking. Only I get a good look at you, and when I talk to the authorities there are three of you, all men. Peet and Chinske will back me up. They'll swear to any description I give, and they'll even believe it."

It could work. But Cord didn't like the idea of relying on Jasperson.

"You trust us?" Cord said. "You figure we'll even bother to leave your share?"

"If you don't, I could suddenly remember what you really look like and who you are. The color of your horses too, and what you wore and where you were heading. I'll put up five thousand for you dead or alive. Maybe we can all share the same cell."

"I don't like you enough," Chi said.

"I don't blame you. I'm an adulterer, an embezzler, a conspirator, and with any luck I'll soon be an accessory to bank robbery. I married a woman I despise for her money, and I've got as much financial sense as a steer has balls. I don't like me much these days either. But none of us has to like me. All we have to do is rob my bank."

A week later, they did.

It came off just as banker Jasperson said. On the way out of town they left his share in a strongbox under a yucca, forty paces from where a granite spire marked a bend in the desert trail. Four days later in Barstow, Cord read an article headlined DESPERADOES SAVAGE LAS VEGAS BANK, bylined "A Correspondent," in the Carson City *Register*. Jasperson had provided the law with a detailed description of three outlaws and was praised for his coolness under duress. Kermit Chinske was sorry he had not gotten a good look at any of the men, but Arla Peet was able to note that the leader was a coarse, pock-marked man, and that one of the others appeared to be part Negro. All Mrs. Peet could recall of the third man was that he walked with a limp.

Cord and Chi moved west to the California coast, then

south around Los Angeles. They settled for a few days to rest themselves and the horses, but Cord could not relax. "Why are you like this?" Chi asked one afternoon as they stared out at the Pacific. "Just when things are going well."

But this feeling was an old story with Cord. "I start wondering, is all. About what is coming next, and so on."

But they were on a run of luck not even Cord's moodiness could queer. On their third day near Los Angeles, Chi came into a barroom where Cord was dawdling over a shot of bourbon whiskey. She took him over to a corner table, sat him down, and slapped the previous day's edition of the Los Angeles *Call* in front of him. She looked happy as he'd ever seen her.

The article was on the third page. Purley Morrison and Lon Bender, both of whom were awaiting execution by the State of California for multiple convictions on rape and murder charges, had agreed to reveal where the proceeds of the Durango Wells Fargo job were hidden. In Durango, the *Call* reminded its readers, nearly $100,000 in currency and pay-to-bearer notes drawn on the Federal Government were stolen. Morrison and Bender's information was accurate. The loot was recovered and Morrison's and Bender's sentences were commuted to life at hard labor.

Cord read the last paragraph three times. Cord and Chi were named, their accurate ages given. They were no longer connected to the Durango job, and the Federal warrants for their arrests were quashed.

"Drinks are on me, *chico*," Chi said, and she went off to the bar for bourbon and a bottle of tequila for herself.

It meant they could move around more or less freely for the first time in two years. They were still wanted in a couple of states, but it was the Federal warrant that had been insidiously dangerous. They had been fair game anywhere for any random bounty hunter. Now they could travel most any trail they wanted, and their saddlebags were full of money.

They drank that night, and agreed without much talk that it was time to settle for a spell and draw some deep breaths. The next day they headed south, then east to Yuma and the bad-water stage road across the Sonora Desert to Tucson. When they reached Juárez it seemed mostly comfortable, and for a couple of weeks their days revolved around the drowsy dark beer on the patio of *Los Tres Hermanos*.

But even Juárez was a wary compromise. They were both too close to what had once been home. Cord was maybe five hundred miles from the farmlands where his father had plowed away his life, and the sense of Texas running off endlessly to the east brought Cord occasional twinges of sadness which didn't seem to have much to do with remorse over his life, but with something deeper and darker and more obscure. These feelings would settle on Cord any time he slowed down more than a few days, the old memories getting loose from the bottom of his mind like the bogeymen of childhood.

Cord remembered his father's eyes going dull as river-stones, darkening and sinking back into the hollows beneath his brows as the seasons of planting and thin harvest went their cycles. His father was an old man—had always been an old man, unable to imagine any better life and unable to escape as Cord had, riding away on one of his father's horses. His father had died not long after, and his mother a few years later—and Cord had tried to deaden his memories of them. Usually it worked, but in the first few days in Juárez during the late sundown afternoon with a little too much of the Mexican beer in his belly, Cord would see his father clear: thickened and coarsened by his labors, rarely communicating beyond nodding and gesturing, as if even speech had failed him.

That kind of farming had been walking death, so Cord never regretted leaving; it was the only way to save himself. Still, those memories saddened him. He figured he knew the problem: Something inside him was judging his life as cold and selfish, however unfair that might be. Yet he could not resolve the feeling. Maybe it would wear away, in time.

Cord knew his choices were harder than any his father ever made, but he was capable of such choices, and his father never was. And because of that—his strength—Cord could have done more to save his people than he liked to admit, surely more than he had ever attempted.

Cord wondered about Chi: Did this northern Mexico country touch her as it did him? She wasn't any farther from the State of Durango than he was from East Texas. He knew her people had been ranchers on some great spread of property, and that her brother was killed near Mexico D.F. in 1867 when he was very young, while fighting for Benito Juárez and Mexican liberty against the Austrian imposter Emperor Maximilian. He knew little more about her past, but she was quiet as well on those late afternoons, and Cord wondered what she was seeing in her mind's eye, what her sadness might be, and what she had turned away from to join him in outlaw ways.

But now, sitting on the patio of the *Hermanos* on the day after Christmas, Cord sw again that such misgivings did not matter much. There was no profit in dwelling on any past which was gone beyond recovery.

Maybe a half hour had passed since Deputy Thomas Bowen had left them alone, and neither had spoken in that time. Chi was watching the children bunched around the crèche, staring with total absorption. But Cord knew she was waiting for answers.

Just then he did not feel like offering them. "It goes back a long ways," he said instead.

"Yeah. And it sure catches up."

Fifty miles off west the sun was touching the ridge of the Potrillo range, rays cutting between the jagged peaks. The animals within the fence on the plaza were gathered around a mound of hay someone had forked for them. A woman's voice called from somewhere, and the children straggled reluctantly away. Then they were gone, and except for an old man on a bench across the park everyone had gone to seek an evening meal.

"*Qué dice?*" Chi said, watching the old man.

"I owe him. I guess you already figured."

"Kinsolving."

"Right. He did me a turn a long time ago, before you and I hooked up. So now I've got to see what he wants."

She would finish the beer before her, Chi thought, then have one shot of tequila to clear the bitter taste. She would return to the *fonda* where they were staying, and the *mesero's* son would bring hot water and she would soak in the tub for a time. They would find a café and take a long while eating supper—beans and rice and roast pork with chile sauce, *rojo y verde*. Maybe after that they would talk.

"When I've taken care of this Kansas business—whatever it is—we can meet up back here." Cord seemed intensely interested in the wet circles the bottom of his beer glass left on the tabletop. "If you want to move out beforehand, leave word with the *cantinera*. I might be gone some time."

He drained the glass. "Could be there isn't much to it. Could be that Kinsolving—"

"Cord," Chi interrupted.

He looked at her.

"I'm going with you."

Cord studied the tabletop again. "You've never been to west Kansas in the winter. It's a two-week ride from here, and at its end you are dead in the heart of nowhere. The winds come off the slope of the Rockies, which gives them a couple hundred miles to get up speed, and nothing—no hills or canyons or trees—nothing to slow them down. They come screaming across the prairie, drifting snow man-deep against anything upright, cutting into your skin like broken glass."

"And there is Kinsolving," Chi said.

"Right. Whatever he wants, I figure it's trouble."

"We're used to that."

"I got to go," Cord said stubbornly. "You don't."

"Yeah," Chi said. "I do."

For a time she had been feeling uneasy when away from him, and the bracelet he gave her, along with his delight in the gold watch, told her it was mutual. In some degree his melancholy had to do with something that happened last summer up in the gold-camp country of the Dakota Territory. Cord had been forced into killing a man he respected and even liked. There had been no escaping, but when it was over Cord drank for two weeks and then announced he was quitting the gunhand game. "This life is nothing but a goddamned slaughterhouse," he had said, and there was considerable truth to it. She helped him through that, and she meant to help him through this new buiness.

"Cord," Chi said. "We don't talk about this any more tonight. There will be time enough tomorrow, and on the trail."

Cord held his quiet. Across the plaza the old man got up and walked stiffly away. They were completely alone together for the last few moments of Juárez sunset.

Chapter Three

THE BREEZE CAME UP THE MORNING THEY waded their horses across the chill Arkansas River. It was steady enough to loft the snow flurries so they stuck to Cord's eyelashes and two-week growth of stubble. Near Trinidad in southern Colorado he'd bought a winter coat from an old Comanche woman. It was fashioned of calf's leather lined with three inches of yellow lamb's wool, with a high collar Cord had turned up above his ears, and elkhorn buttons held in place with rawhide loops. His boots were new, and his feet ached because of the extra socks he was wearing, but it was better than freezing; nothing was worse than cold feet horseback. He wore new yellow buckskin gloves and his neckerchief pulled over his nose and mouth, so he looked like some kind of dime-novel road agent. And still he was cold.

Chi rode with her head bent into the breeze, dressed as always in serape and sombrero. If the sharp chill bothered her, she did not show her discomfort.

The first mapmakers had ignored this vast flatland, labeling it the Great American Desert. Maybe that was not far wrong. Anyway, it was mostly country to travel through, toward the old Southwest or the gold camps like Leadville in the Rockies, and surely no place to live on any long-term basis. But people had finally homesteaded even here,

21

digging wells by hand until they either struck water or the walls caved in and buried them alive—as the country would eventually. Later they cut ditches from the rivers with horse-drawn Fresno scrapers, and raised wind-whipped gardens. God bless those homesteaders, Cord thought. They could have it all, far as he was concerned.

From his earliest days away from home and trailing longhorns north to the railheads, Kansas had meant territory to be reached. Each year the railroad moved west, first Topeka and then Junction City; Abilene in '71; Hays; and at the end, Newton and Dodge City. Three months on the trail at thirty dollars per, with a ten-dollar bonus for sticking it out through runoff rivers, beef-hungry Indians, coyotes and stampedes and four hours' sleep a night, meals of beans and greasy bacon eaten on the go, and bridging across the quicksand on the trunks of fallen trees. And the dust. More than any single thing Cord recalled the dust. Eating it on the trail and tasting it in the food, always gritting between your teeth.

And finally the railhead town and a hell-raising welcome. The beef buyers from Chicago and Philadelphia and New York were always happy to see the herds come rolling in. The cows they bought for fifteen dollars a head would be worth three or four times that much back East, so the buyers always did their best to entertain the drovers, concealing whatever distaste they might have had for the wild-assed unshaven Texas boys who were seeing their first real money and town, and sometimes buying their first grown-up women.

Cord and the kind of boys he rode with always ended up in Texas Town—every railhead had a Texas Town, across the tracks where the invading drovers could spend their money on sin out of sight of proper folks. Cord played some at poker and bucked the tiger at faro because it was expected

He would have liked it better if they were willing to talk. In those days his conversation was mostly around the tailgate of some chuckwagon, and it was never enough. It ran to too-often-told tales of ladies that were as stylized as Greek epics, or pious declarations about how after this drive, for sure, one hand or another was going to take his pay and settle down.

But the women would not talk at all. Once Cord had even offered to pay one for talk and nothing else. She was suspicious, and asked if he wouldn't like to tie her up instead. Then when she saw he was serious, she laughed. As he was leaving, Cord heard her telling the story to the others.

So Kansas had always been something of a disappointment.

"*Muchacho,*" Chi called over her shoulder. "How far?"

"Bowen," the deputy said. He was a horselength back. "The name is Bowen."

"*Sí, Muchacho* Bowen. How far?"

They reined up and Bowen came alongside, scanning the sky. It was the uniform color of gunmetal, and they could see no more than a couple hundred yards through the flurries of ground blizzard this late afternoon. Cord checked his new watch: just after four.

"Four, maybe five hours," Bowen said. "Unless something slows us."

"Not tonight," Cord said.

"We'll make it if we keep moving."

"This is poor country for wandering in the cold dark of night. No stars and no trees, so everything starts to look like you've seen it before."

"Not if you know these parts."

"One more night," Chi said.

Bowen was a puzzle so far. On the trail he almost never

spoke, except to answer questions, and Cord voiced few of those. As to Kinsolving and his town of Weed, and why he'd called for Cord to ride more than six hundred miles in the dead of winter, Cord figured that would be revealed in time.

But Cord had to wonder what this young deputy had to do with all this. Bowen had only mentioned Kinsolving by name that one time on the patio of the *Hermanos*, with anger and frustration and respect all mixed up in his tone. Yet once the message was delivered the deputy showed little interest in whether Cord came or not. That last evening in Juárez, while Chi had her bath, Cord searched Bowen out to tell him they would be ready to ride at dawn. Cord was surprised to see a quick flash of impatience and anger cross Bowen's features before he said, "I'll be ready," in a flat voice.

Now Bowen walked his horse forward, pointed off into the swirling snow, and said, "Look there."

"Smoke," Chi said. "You can smell it."

Cord could not. He moved the bay gelding up beside Bowen. The even, snow-covered ground and the slate of spackled sky blended in an indistinct horizon. Cord saw the shadowy forms of a few willows in a draw where a creek likely ran through, at least part of the year. Then he did smell the smoke, and spotted a dark mass against the far creekbank, a cabin, with the sooty line streaming toward them in a thin breeze-driven meander which quickly dissipated among the snowfall.

"Some grass-buster holed up for the winter," Cord suggested.

"No," Bowen said. "That soddy has been empty two seasons."

"Who then?" Chi wondered aloud.

"Let's find out," Cord said, nudging the gelding forward.

"Hold up," Bowen said sharply.

Cord turned in the saddle and said, "We've got to spend one more night on the trail. If you got some reason for spending it under a tree and not beside that fire, you say it."

"Call it a hunch."

"Too cold for hunches," Cord said, and he rode for the soddy.

He reined up in front. The blocks of cut sod were piled on three sides to form walls, roofed by crossed planks topped with more sod. A stovepipe with a little conical topper poked through. The door was a three-by-three gap in the front wall covered with a tattered blanket.

Cord cupped his hands and hollered, "Hello, the soddy!"

The voices of more than one man rose inside, but no one answered. Cord called again.

The blanket was pushed aside, and the snow pasted to it sifted to the ground. The man who came out wore a buffalo robe and carried an old Henry .44 rifle. He worked the lever-action and held the muzzle pointed somewhere in front of the bay gelding. Chi and Tom Bowen rode up on either side of Cord.

"Shit," Bowen muttered. "Sure as sunup, you could bet money on something like this."

"Whaddya want?" the man with the Henry growled.

"A night's shelter."

"Find it somewhere else. We got no room."

There was no such thing as no room, not on open prairie in this sort of weather. That was only common decency.

"Ride on," the man with the Henry snapped.

"I don't think so," Chi said. Her Colt Peacemaker was in her hand, the long barrel steady on the man with the Henry.

The man grinned and licked his lips. "You don't need to

shoot your way in. Not you, lady. You'd be right welcome, is my guess." He looked at Cord and stopped smiling. "The rest of you can go to hell. There is nine more men inside, and unless you reckon you can gun them all, you are sleeping with nature tonight."

"We'll ride on," Cord said.

Chi put her hand on his reins. "Cord."

"Maybe there are nine more men in there," Cord said wearily. "Maybe not. It doesn't matter. None of this is worth gunplay."

"I say we ride." It was Bowen.

Chi glared at the deputy. "We are being buffaloed," she said, looking angry and exceedingly handsome in the dusky light.

"Yeah," Cord said. "That happens."

A second man made his way through the low door and straightened beside the man with the Henry. He was a head shorter, compactly built except for a hint of gut over his gunbelt. He had a thin, clean-shaven, lupine face and wore spectacles which magnified his eyes.

"My name is Con James," he announced. "This here is my bunch."

"You ought to teach this one some manners," Chi said.

James stared at her blankly. "Step down if you want. Our horses are down by the creek. There's water that isn't froze over, and the willows give some windbreak."

But as they walked back from tethering their mounts with the other animals, Cord had the uncomfortable feeling that what had begun as his idea had twisted into someone else's play.

The soddy was not much bigger than a single hotel room. In its middle was a rusty cast-iron woodstove, fire glowing red around the gap where the door did not quite close. A white-enameled coffeepot, filthy with crusted grounds, sat atop, and a coal-oil lamp hung from a hook in one of the roof planks, casting sooty fingers of shadow toward the soddy's corners.

After the bite of cold the room was too hot, the smoke of cigarettes and the poorly vented stove thick enough to burn the eyes. Cord found a spot in one corner, dropped his saddlebags, and slumped to sit on them. Near the dirt floor the air was cooler and cleaner.

The ten men in the room stank. They smelled of sweat and horses, of spoiled food and rotten teeth, of urine and filthy union suits. But there was another, darker odor of tension which touched Cord's nostrils like ozone. Chi's presence had to have something to do with it. It was odds-on these men had not seen a woman for a good long time.

"I got tobacco to trade for coffee," Cord said. He tossed out his pouch, and Con James snatched it out of the air. With elaborate casualness he rolled a smoke and lit it with a lucifer he struck on the hot metal of the stove. He passed it to the next man, who gestured to Cord with it like he was proposing a toast.

Cord dug his cup from his saddlebag, filled it and handed it to Chi. The look she gave told him she also recognized the man with the pouch.

His name was Jasey Crook. When they had last crossed paths, he was working out of Fort Benton, Montana Territory, rustling horses and driving them north into Canada fdor resale.

Cord filled another cup for himself and one for Bowen. The deputy looked down into his and said nothing. Crook was not only the only familiar face in this bunch. The little bandy-legged black Irishman in the corner was named Mac Cobb, and the slim black man with the outsized hands called himself Digger Dean. On the far side sat a huge man with a full beard split by teeth bared in an unpleasant grin. This was Reuben C. Greyson, mostly noteworthy for bullying and cowardice and chicken-livered stalling, a rank item even among this company.

A fine bunch of thugs, Cord thought, *all holed up only miles from where we are headed.* Greyson drank deeply from a whiskey bottle and passed it on. It was not the only bottle going the rounds.

The thing that made sense was to get up and get out. Time would pass slowly in this fetid dugout. Cord and Chi and Bowen had spent nights in the open lately, and could suffer another. What stopped Cord was the idea of this gang thinking they had bluffed him out. Maybe that was stupid, worrying about that sort of mindless bullying and backing down—but still, Cord stayed.

Chi sat next to him with her back to the wall, knees drawn up and hands hidden under her serape. Her sombrero was down over her face. Somehow she had always been able to retreat into sleep.

Tom Bowen sat at Cord's other hand. He was using his knife to scrape the last beans from a tin, hardly looking at the food, his eyes darting around the room instead. His jaws moved in determined rhythms, chewing only a mechanical preliminary to swallowing, and no enjoyment to it.

Cord liked nothing about being in this room. James had it staked out like a snake's den.

Some of the others were also eating, gnawing at strips of jerky tough as saddle leather, or using fingers or knives on tinned beans. One man plucked the last fruit from a can of pears, then poured whiskey into the syrup. Con James would watch Cord a spell, then look ostentatiously away, like this was the preliminary to some contest. Maybe it was.

Cord rose. Bowen and the James bunch studied him as if at any moment he might fly to the moon, though Chi did not stir. Cord crouched and made his way through the low door.

Around on the leeward side of the soddy he undid his britches and pissed into a snowdrift. Nearby there was a pile of trash: empty tins, stove ashes, scraps of oiled paper smeared with food stains. The pile was fresh, not yet scavenged over by varmints. James and his bunch had been holed up here a couple of days at most.

The bay gelding nickered when Cord approached out of the blowing snow. Where the horse was tied, the creek bent, casting a riffle which kept a little of the water open, and the gelding had been pawing for grass. It was days since their mounts had been grained, and Cord considered turning the gelding loose on a long tether, hobbled. But that was probably a bad idea; could be they would want to move on in a hurry. Cord had chosen the big horse for stamina, and there would be plenty of grain another day.

Behind the willow windbreak Cord rolled a smoke from the pouch he'd retrieved, and managed to get it lit. He had not smoked in the soddy because he could not stomach the thought of the taste tainted by the smell of those men.

The place was set to blow, Cord figured. Any ten men crammed into that dark space not big enough for two would get on each other's nerves, but James's kind were always looking for trouble. Pen them up like this and they would be carving on each other before long.

Which meant James expected to turn them loose soon. When he did, the brutality would not be pretty. Cord also had to deal with the possibility that Kinsolving had called him here to confront this rubbish.

Someone laughed inside the dugout, loud enough for Cord to hear above the wind's whine. It was a nasty sound having nothing to do with mirth.

Cord stopped outside the blanketed door long enough to hear someone say, "You got a big mouth, Reuben Greyson.

Betcha that is all you got that's big. Betcha you're a baby where it counts."

"Fuck you," Reuben Greyson said.

The other man laughed the kind of laugh that is supposed to grate on a man and rankle him into doing something which will provoke more laughter. "You said it, Reuben. You'd screw a blind heifer if you had one around. But women, how about women? You ever screw a woman? Or can you remember?"

Other men laughed. Cord pushed through the blanket.

Reuben Greyson stood wiping his mouth on his sleeve, as if this might make his mind work better. He was staring across at Chi, who had not moved. Tom Bowen was in a far corner, and Mac Cobb stood over him, holding a revolver.

"That's far enough, mister." Con James had his own gun on Cord. "Stand easy, and this will be over before you know it."

"You going to do her?" Digger Dean needled from the shadow of the stove. "You going to show her a real man?"

"Shut up, nigger." But Greyson sounded sick.

"That's the way," Digger said. "Start with me. Fighting is easier than fucking anyway, 'specially for a dickless white boy like you."

Con James was watching the fun, so Cord could have gone for his own gun. But clean gunplay in this room would be impossible. A few shots and the air would be opaque with black-powder smoke, and the rest would be random lead-slinging. Drawing down was not the play, at least not yet.

Bowen's gaze flicked from man to man, as if he were awaiting his chance. Cord hoped to hell the young deputy would have the sense to let this work itself out. From the beginning on the patio of the *Hermanos*, Cord had seen something volatile in Bowen. He was angered beyond reason by something deeply felt, or impatient, as if life had best start going as he thought it should and damned soon, or he would take steps to remedy the situation.

Chi still had not moved, nor given indication she was anything but asleep.

"You know where to put it?" Digger ragged. "You just spread her open, see, and there's this hole. Probably wet as a swamp and just waiting for your little white thing, Reuben."

"Yeah," Greyson said in the tones of a child. He came around the glowing stove to stand over Chi, the toes of his boots almost touching hers. Still she did not move.

"Put the feel to her, Reuben," Digger said. "Git her all lathered up."

Greyson looked down to Chi and said, "Hey!"

Chi did not move.

Cord watched Greyson realize he was backed into a corner. He was expected to do something, and he did not know how to go about it.

"You Mex bitch," he growled. "You look at me."

Chi brought up her left hand very slowly, tilted back her sombrero, and eyed Greyson.

Greyson smiled and reached with both hands for the buttons on his britches. "Get ready, cunt."

Chi's right hand appeared and her Colt was in it, the hammer back on full cock and the barrel just grazing Greyson's crotch, six inches beneath his hands, now frozen on his buttons. Cord had seen her speed so many times, and yet it was always new and marvelous, those hands that were faster than thought.

Greyson moaned.

Con James was paying Cord no mind at all now, but Cord kept still. There was no need.

Chi raised her chin in an abrupt gesture and Greyson's

hands shot up above his shoulders. As Chi stood, her gun never wavered, a fraction of an inch from his manhood, like the breath of a woman.

"What did you call me?"

Chi's tone was soft, as if she were genuinely curious.

Reuben Greyson shot a look over his shoulder. None of the others gave any sign of backing his play, and Greyson knew his chances were screwed. In the chalky whiteness of his face was the vision of cupping his hands and finding nothing but bloody torn pulp where his cock and balls had hung, the shock of gunfire and the warm blood on his fingers as he tried to stop himself from dying.

"Tell me," Chi said. "Tell me once more."

Someone snickered. It did not matter to these men: Rape and killing were versions of the same thing, seeing someone hurt. They loved any bloodiness, as long as it was not theirs.

"You going to say it?" Chi's tone was soft, almost seductive. "You going to tell me what I am, *puerco?*" Then her voice went to ice, chill as Greyson's fear.

"What am I?" Chi hissed.

Greyson licked cracked lips and whispered, "Cunt."

Chi's arm moved no more than six inches, the barrel of her Peacemaker stabbing into Greyson's groin. The bearded man screamed like a woman and grabbed himself, hunching over with pain. Chi stepped back and Greyson staggered a step before falling across the hot stove. He screamed and fishtailed away to drop to the dirt floor, where he lay curled up like a child, his face contorted in anguish and soft mewling sounds coming from his mouth.

"My Lordy, Mister Greyson," Digger Dean drawled. "Looks like she stuck you before you could stick her. Looks like her tool is harder than yours."

Chi swung her Colt on the black. "Watch your mouth,

negro. Killing you would be free. No one would care."

"I'm quiet," Dean said. "I never could get it up for strangers."

But that sort of taunt was old news, and Chi let it go. Con James nodded to her, as if everything was going to work out fine after all. He holstered his gun and said, "Somebody pass that damned bottle."

Cord stepped over Greyson and the bearded man managed to twist and look up at him. "I'll get you, you bastard. You and that . . . you and her both. You see if I don't."

Cord kicked Greyson in the ribs, hard enough to bring a fresh moan. No one objected. "No, you won't," Cord said. "You just made a heavy threat, and I'm going to kill you for it, right now." Cord drew his Peacemaker and shoved the barrel into Greyson's face. "It's simpler this way," he said reasonably. "I kill you, and I don't have to worry about you shooting me in the back some night." Cord grinned as Greyson's face turned babyish, the blustering swallowed by primal, lip-trembling fear.

"But I guess not," Cord said. "It would be like killing a child. But the next time you come around, the lady will likely shoot, and you won't be a man anymore, if you ever were one. The lady will cut off your cock and pickle it and wear it around her neck on a string, for show. You see if she doesn't."

Cord eased his revolver back into its holster and turned to Chi. "You all right?" he asked as he eased down next to her.

"What the hell do you think?" Chi snapped. There was color high up on her olive cheeks. This sort of thing happened every now and then, but she never got used to it, and he did not expect she ever would. Men like Greyson were more interested in humiliation than sex, and her pride was an edge she would kill for.

Greyson dragged himself off into the shadows.

Chi did not speak again, and Cord had sense enough to stay quiet. The hard glower remained on her face, and the men in the dugout could not meet it for long, looking quickly away, grabbing for one of the bottles. After a time they began to curl up for sleep, snorting, and the ones with broken noses sometimes gagging, drunk and sprawled together like animals.

Cord lay out his own bedroll beside Chi, so she was between him and the wall. She was already wrapped in her serape and lying still, but when he pulled his blanket over himself, she stirred. Then he felt her nestle against his back, settling and adjusting and molding the curve of her body to his until she was comfortable. Cord stiffened, utterly bemused. In all their years together she had never come to him like this, and he wondered how much it had to do with their good times in Juárez, or how much she was shaken by Greyson. Maybe she was only cold.

Her breath was warm on his neck and he could feel the softness of her breasts rising and falling as she drifted toward sleep. Presently Cord began to relax. The fire in the stove burned down to a few red embers among gray coals, and finally Cord drifted away to sleep filled with dreams he would not remember.

Chapter Four

T HEY WERE HORSEBACK THE NEXT MORNING before the late winter dawn, and the day when it came was a faint lightening of the night. The snow and wind had picked up while they slept, dry brittle flakes slanting across the trail before them. Visibility was down to maybe fifty yards. Beyond that everything—the softly undulating drifts, the frosted scrub brush, the close cloudy sky—everything took on a canescent sameness.

Bowen was leading them along a double-rutted wagon trace that cut straight across the flatlands. Judging from the absence of tracks, no one had passed this way for at least a day. In this country, sensible people would keep close to shelter and fire through these weeks of the worst season.

Cord brought up the rear. Every so often the wind would break or shift, and through the veil of eddying snow he saw the fences or ditches that signified the presence of nearby farms and ranches. Once a dairy cow lowed, lost somewhere in the coming storm, and Cord wondered if she would survive. This was mostly wheat and feed-corn country, and the man who owned her was probably housebound. A ways back Cord had made out one frame-and-plank cabin with a little porch, but most of the dwellings they had passed were soddies not much bigger than the one in which they had spent the night, the seed-head grass on the roofs dull brown in the wind. Nearby were willowthatch corrals, and sometimes a barn or storage shed dug into a hillslope, and always, out back, a privy.

The day hung so near to twilight Cord could see the faint lights of cookstoves and coal-oil lanterns shining through the tiny windows. How would it be to live this way, he wondered, hunkered against the winter for months at a time? How did these people pass the days? Cord saw pale-skinned men and women from the north of Europe, eyes squinty from smoke and reading in the constant dimness, the same three books again and again. He saw them sitting hours over checkers or Patience, mending clothes that did not need mending, and making love while the children tried not to watch and the cold drafts of air cutting through the walls teased at bare skin. East Texas had been bad enough, even without the cold, so Cord had seen enough of such life to know it was like going to jail voluntarily, waiting and static, and living amid thoughts that twisted into strange ropes before the world turned green again. It could lead to the ugliest kid of craziness, where men chopped off their offending peckers with hatchets, and despairing women smothered their crying children.

Summer would not be much better in this country: prayer for two hours on Sunday, and work every other waking moment. Winter snow would break into cold rain. There would be one or two glorious weeks of spring in early May, the trees bursting to leaf—but then the sun-blinded days of field labor began and would not seem to end, sweat and dust and muscle-wrenching toil for a few bushels of wheat or oats or barley from each homestead acre. Unless the year brought fire, or grasshoppers, or the creeks and ditches were dry, and everything withered and went dead as the dirt.

These people had been lured west by the railroads with promises of land and easy wealth, and melons on every vine. The railroads got rich, and the homesteaders got dryland farming and this wind and snow, silence and isolation and an increasing sense of having failed themselves, their children, their dreams. You had to be stupid to stay, Cord thought, and immediately wondered if that was too easy for him to say, an easy-rider in life, taking and never giving. What would he think of himself when he was old and ready for dying? That was what this country did: It drove the mind to pointless meanderings.

The wagon trace climbed a slight grade. Tom Bowen sat his horse at the crest. When they reached him they saw that the slope fell away gently to a wide swale. Frigid wind slapped at the side of Cord's head, and his gelding sidestepped, snorting and prancing in his urgency to find cover. Then the wind died some, and Cord and Chi saw the town of Weed.

Here was the nesters' marketplace. They would come in the spring for provisions and in the fall to sell their produce and stock their larders for another numbing winter. Of the six buildings, the only two-story structure was the mercantile, now dark as a vault. The upstairs would hold a couple of rooms only used a few weeks in the fall by the visiting grain buyers. Facing the mercantile was the county sheriff's office, with its barred side windows. Behind it were two cabins, one a little smaller than the other. Toward the far end of Weed, set off enough so the odor of horseshit would not reek everywhere, was the livery barn with corrals behind. Somewhere not far away there would be grain elevators. Cord knew these towns.

The rail station and telegraph office was at the end of the little street, set, like the tracks, perpendicular to the rest of the layout. The Western Union agent would handle what banking the people of Prine County had. The railway ran straight as a gunshot east and west to vanish in the grayness way short of any horizon; it was paralleled by a line of poles carrying the double-strand of the telegraph wire. Beyond the tracks, Coffee River meandered through the prairie lands, discernible now only as an unvaried wide path of smooth, snow-covered ice.

"Fine-looking town," Cord said.

"Yeah," Chi said. "Sure pleased to be here."

"Must get to jumping," Cord said, "come late August or so, with the three-legged races and the quilting bees—the whole shitaree." A faint light showed from the barred windows of the jailhouse, the only sign of habitation. *Except for the ghosts*, Cord thought. There were always ghosts in places like these, conjured up by too much time and winter-warped imagination.

Bowen scowled. "This does it for me," he said, "soon as I show you in. Let's get that done."

"*Sí, muchacho*," Chi said gravely. Bowen's scowl deepened, and he wheeled his horse and spurred down the final easy slope. Cord saw that Chi liked something in the dark-natured deputy; otherwise she would not have bothered to tease him.

The wind kicked up as they neared the town, and without warning they were enveloped in a cloud of snow so thick Cord felt momentarily unmoored. He reined up to let it pass.

From out of the snow's swirl emerged a figure. Cord leaned across the gelding's neck, peered into the drifting flurries.

Then the snow cloud passed, and Cord saw it was a girl, maybe fifteen years old. She was hatless; her hair was long, stringy, the color of the dead winter grass, and snarled and tangled as a robin's nest. The girl wore a random assortment of ill-fitting clothing: a long loose skirt patched over several times with scraps that did not match, high-button shoes, a short quilted jacket over a sweater with holes showing a second sweater beneath. Several shirt collars sprouted up like windflowers above the torn scrap of scarf around her neck.

The girl stood motionless as a moonstruck calf in the middle of the street before the mercantile, staring up at them through dark, pellucid eyes.

On down in front of the sheriff's office, Tom Bowen had climbed off his horse and stood, waiting, watching.

The raggedy girl eyed Cord and took a stumbling step away, but then she saw Chi. Her mouth came soundlessly open. She stared up at the dark horsewoman, and wonderment overcame her apprehension.

Chi leaned forward and shouted above the wind, "What are you doing in the storm, *niña?* Go home to your mother."

The girl's eyes were riveted on Chi, and Cord sensed his partner was touched by this eerie attention.

"Where is your mama, *muchacha?*"

Bowen had taken a few steps back toward them. "She hasn't got a mother. No kin at all." He sounded angered by the idea.

"Where does she stay?"

"The livery, mostly. She makes out. They call her Aggie."

"Aggie," Chi repeated. "Come here, Aggie." The girl stayed put, so Chi stepped her horse ahead a few paces, then reached a hand down to the child. Her serape fell loose as she bent, revealing her holster.

The girl's eyes fixed on Chi's long-barreled Colt. Then she whirled and dashed away. In a moment she was swallowed by the storm, like a snow-blind hallucination.

Chi turned a blank look on Cord. He shook his head impatiently. This strange child with the depthless eyes had nothing to do with the business at hand—at least he hoped she did not. He rode past Chi to the hitching rail in front of the sheriff's office and tethered the gelding beside Bowen's horse. A lamp glowed through the front window.

John P. Kinsolving had heard them ride in. He stood behind his desk, unconsciously flexing the fingers of his right hand. Cord came through the door and stepped to one side, and Chi and Bowen followed.

"I figured you would come," Kinsolving said. "I was counting on it."

"I bet you were, John P."

Kinsolving looked to be carrying a considerable weight of years and hard living on his rounded shoulders. He was a big man, at six and a half feet some five inches taller than Cord. At one time Kinsolving's stature had been a presence. Now it was only bulk, as if too much man had been layered onto a normal frame. His gunbelt, worn soft and smooth as calfskin over the years, hung below an overlapping gut, and his nose was big and doughy and chased with broken capillaries, as if he and Jim Beam were old nighttime conferees. Kinsolving's eyes were sunken and dulled, and framed with deep leathery creases.

His left arm was wrong: hanging loose, the palm of his hand faced forward. Cord knew the elbow was twisted from a break which was never set, so Kinsolving could not fully extend it. The sheriff wore a faded woolen shirt buttoned to the neck, and over it a dark leather vest with his silver star pinned on one panel. His feet were lapping out of scuffed slippers.

Cord, in new boots and coat, felt vaguely abashed, as if his prosperity was in some measure responsible for the other man's deterioration.

"This calls for a drink." Kinsolving pulled open the top drawer of his desk and brought out a bottle and glasses.

"That's what we'll do," he said, as if there had been some question. "We'll have us a drink."

"I been on the trail the better part of two months," Tom Bowen said evenly. "I've done what was asked of me." He went past Kinsolving and through a door behind the desk. He would live in the smaller of the two cabins out back, and Kinsolving in the other.

Kinsolving stared a moment at the door after Bowen shut it behind him. "Sit down," he said. "Make yourselves to home."

The captain's chair Cord took had two missing back slats. Chi's rocked on uneven legs. Kinsolving splashed amber whiskey into three glasses, and slid two across the desk. "To the future," he said, raising his.

Cord drank and said nothing. Kinsolving's flush told Cord this was not the sheriff's first snort of the morning.

"You ever hear from Carson Sheeny?" Kinsolving asked.

"Not for twelve years."

"We had us some times, you and me and him." Kinsolving shook his head and ran his tongue over the front of his upper bridge, savoring either the memory or that day's breakfast. Carson Sheeny had been shot in the back by a seventeen-year-old town constable in Independence, Missouri, nearly ten years before.

Kinsolving picked up the bottle, but Cord put two fingers over his glass and shook his head no. Kinsolving poured for himself and Chi. "What'll we drink to, miss?"

"Success to crime," Chi said.

Kinsolving laughed, too loud and too long.

"It isn't too bad," he said, gesturing toward the bottle. "Shopkeeper down at the mercantile ran a liquor room up front. He left two months ago, when the snow started in and would not stop. Got to drinking his own wares and came down with the jimjams so bad he up and rode out. Didn't try to sell out or salvage any of his stock, neither. You folks help yourself." Kinsolving poured himself a third shot. "I do."

"Sounds like you got Christmas all winter," Cord said. He wondered what Chi was thinking of all this. She reached across him to fish makings from his shirt pocket.

"I hear Hard Petey Maginnis got run down by a buckboard in North Platte," Kinsolving said.

"Is that so?"

Cord took the cigarette Chi offered. Its smoke spiraled lazily toward the ceiling. Outside the wind had changed pitch, like an opera singer testing her voice. Dust moved along the floor where the draft crept under the door.

"John P.," Cord said, "why don't you cut straight to the point of this?"

Kinsolving looked fondly at his glass but did not pick it up. "I need you, Cord," he told the glass. "There's a job wants doing, and I cannot play a lone hand."

Cord waited.

"You owe me, *amigo.*"

"We all know that," Cord snapped. "No need to flop it out and look it over. I'm here. You tell me why."

Kinsolving flushed red. For months he had waited on this moment, and now he could not speak his piece, at least not straight like a man.

He picked up his glass and followed it with his eyes all the way to his lips. He drank until it was empty and then he grinned, the whiskey burning resolve into his hard-used features.

"You and me, Cord," Kinsolving said. "We are going to rob us a train."

Chapter Five

THE MERCANTILE WAS LIKE SOME KIND OF land-locked Flying Dutchman, condemned to an eternity of Kansas winter. Whatever future the onetime owner had read in the runes of the rough plank flooring must have been dire, and he had fled back to whatever eastern haven he had come from without wasting time putting things to order. Coffee had congealed and then frozen in the pot, and rats had helped themelves to flour from an open bin. Copper pennies were scattered around the floor beneath the open cash drawer, not worth picking up.

The downstairs was divided into two rooms. The larger, in back, was the store proper, a claustrophobic jumble of the necessaries a sodbuster might ask for. One wall was shelves stacked to the ceiling with tinned meat and vegetables, and burlap sacks of rice, corn meal, salt, and dried beans. Another wall featured bolts of yard goods, dull utilitarian lengths of wool and flannel and denim, and one incongruous square yard of fine white lace going gray with dust. A few ready-mades hung on racks: checked shirts, earth-colored britches, and coveralls with riveted seams.

The floor space was a maze of nail kegs, rolled barbed wire, harnesses and tack, rakes and hoes and a single plowblade with no handles. Against the back wall was a long counter cluttered with jars of hard candy and spices.

The lid was off a round tin with a lithograph of Queen Victoria on the side. It held cigars gone so stale they crumbled to dust between Cord's fingers. But he found another covered tin of dark tobacco which was halfway fresh.

In the smaller front room Cord found Chi starting a fire in the fat-bellied cast-iron stove. "There's anything we need back there."

"For what?"

"Whatever."

The onetime mercantilist had the sense to put his liquor business up front, so customers had to pass the temptation of strong drink before they saw to their other needs. This room was no more than fifteen feet to a side and the ceiling was lower. The bar was ten feet of planking across four empty kegs. On the shelf behind were a dozen dirty, chipped glasses, no two alike, and maybe two dozen bottles, all but two unlabeled. No doubt there had been more when the owner left, before Kinsolving got well into his winter drinking. Cord wondered what the sheriff would do if the whiskey ran out before spring.

Chi blew the kindling into flame, then shut the iron door. Beside the stove were two tables, one square and one round. On the round table was a greasy deck of playing cards. Chi sat down and stared off at nothing. She was acting strangely, and Cord thought he knew why.

When they left Kinsolving's office, Cord led the bay gelding and Chi's mare to the livery stable. Three other horses were already stabled there, Bowen's and two rangy geldings which looked to have been both worked in the collar and rode under a saddle. Cord figured they belonged to Kinsolving, signs of poor times and not much pride. Cord unsaddled his bay and the mare, grained them, took his and Chi's saddlebags, and went back out into the cold morning.

There was light showing from under the door of Bowen's cabin, but no sign of the girl Aggie.

The girl: The sight of her and her wild silent fright had stirred Chi in a way Cord had not seen before. He did not know what to make of that.

Cord had dumped their gear in the cold rooms upstairs, each dim as the sea. At least they had fireplaces; they would sleep in some semblance of warmth.

Now, downstairs in the barren liquor room, Chi roused herself to say, "Well now, Mister Cord. What have we got here?"

"Don't have a clue."

"Something," Chi said. "Something I don't like."

Cord wished he could put aside the rules of obligation and debt and ride out with Chi and the money they were packing, back to Juárez and warm afternoons with the good Mexican beer. But by his lights that was simply not an alternative. You paid your debts; that was a rule. So Kinsolving owned his loyalty for this little while.

"There are already too many players in this hand," Cord said. "Con James and that crowd of hoodlums stinking up that soddy. Bowen comes into it too. God knows how it fits together."

"How long?" Chi said.

Cord frowned. "Huh?"

"How long have you owed him?"

"Twelve years."

"He was a *viejo* even then?"

"Not altogether." Cord had been thinking about those days all the ride north, and now it was time Chi knew about it. But before he could begin a gust of wind caught the heavy door and slammed it all the way around into the wall. Aggie stood framed in the opening, her spooked eyes fixed on Chi. She was shivering.

"Come in, *niña*," Chi said gently. She came around the bar toward the girl, and the girl moved to meet her, passing Cord like a sleepwalker. Cord pushed his chair back impatiently, and at the sound the girl jumped away from him. Snow lashed Cord's face when he shut the door.

Chi sat the girl near the stove, but Aggie pulled loose and sat as far from Cord as she could get. Her fingers worried at the frayed material of her skirt. She began to shiver again, so every part of her trembled.

Chi fetched whiskey and a glass, but even with two hands the girl could not hold it without liquor slopping over the table. Chi guided the glass to her mouth. The girl swallowed the smoky whiskey and then shuddered once more, so violently Cord thought she had suffered some sort of seizure. But then she sat immobile, staring at the swaybacked deck of cards.

Chi pushed a matted rope of hair from the girl's pale face, and whispered something Cord could not hear. The girl took Chi's hand in both of hers.

The child spooked Cord; children often did, even if they were not crazy like this one. The trouble was that so many people treated them by special rules, as though youngsters deserved more than they had earned. That went against the code by which Cord lived. He wondered if Chi saw something of herself in this girl, or if she reminded Chi of another child from a faraway Mexico past. Whichever, her instant empathy was as disquieting as the child herself.

"They are out there."

It was the first words the child had spoken.

"Who is out there, *chica?*" Chi asked in the tone she might use to gentle a young horse.

Aggie's huge eyes bored into her. "You saw them. I can tell." She muttered something Cord missed.

"What is she going on about?" he snapped, more sharply than he'd meant.

"'The dark men,'" Chi repeated. "*Diablos?*" she wondered.

"They are out there on the prairie, waiting." Aggie's tone was suddenly almost rational. "You know who I mean. They are coming for us, today or tomorrow or whenever. For all of us, and the old sheriff and the young sheriff and the dark lady."

"What lady?"

Aggie ignored Cord. "We will all disappear, like this." She made a fist, then let her fingers fly open.

"It is all right," Chi murmured.

"Oh, no." Aggie was perfectly calm. "It is not all right."

"Forget it," Cord said, unaccountably angered. "She rode out some time and ran into that crowd in the soddy. Who wouldn't be frightened by those vultures? But there is no need to turn it into some kind of campfire ghost story."

Aggie's hands shot out and she grabbed the open whiskey bottle. She managed two thick swallows before Chi could grab it away. Aggie flinched as if she had been struck. Chi reached for her but Aggie slipped under her hands and scuttled to the door, throwing it open.

Cord swore, and Aggie fixed him with her mad stare. "They will not let you be, you know." Again her voice had gone matter-of-fact. "They will not let you be until you are dead." The girl stepped out into the blowing snow and was gone. Cord blinked twice. He followed Chi out the open door.

They could see nothing but grayness from the boardwalk fronting the store. The street was empty in either direction.

Back inside, Chi shut the door and stood with her back

against it. Her fine features were creased in a thoughtful scowl.

"Well," she said finally, "the *muchacha* had the last part right enough."

Chapter Six

B Y MIDDAY THE SNOW HAD PICKED UP, DRY brittle flakes slanting relentlessly across the street, driven by hard gusts. A drift was piling higher against the front of Kinsolving's office, while some of the street had been blown clear to reveal ruts of frozen mud. Chi drew the thong holding her sombrero tighter, and Cord held the brim of his Stetson with his gloved left hand, ducking his head into the frigid wind.

A path was beaten into the snow from the back door of the sheriff's office to Kinsolving's cabin, a tight log building that told Cord the people of Prine County were once willing to take trouble to attract a good man as sheriff. Kinsolving must have been watching for them, because he swung open the door and squinted out into the blow as they approached.

"Come in," he said. "Shuck the heavy duds and I'll fix us some warming." Uneasiness cut his hearty tone.

Cord shrugged out of the heavy lamb's-wool-lined coat, hung it on a hook near the door, and stomped snow from his boots. Chi looked around the room with open interest, her eyes settling on Kinsolving. He stood it a moment, then rubbed his hands together briskly for no reason and turned away.

In the cabin's front room were a table and four chairs, a sideboard with bare wood showing through worn spots in the varnish, and a low two-shelf bookcase with a Holy Bible and a pile of yellow-covered dime novels. A lamp and a stack of four thick white plates sat on the table, and an unopened whiskey bottle and four glasses on the sideboard, reflecting firelight from the isinglass woodstove door. On the wall between the doors into the back rooms hung a calendar with a colored picture of a proud, prosperous-looking farmer in spotless coveralls standing in front of an endless field of golden wheat. Under the picture, in block letters, was printed SUNSHINE SEED CO., 273 SUMMER STREET, TOPEKA, KANSAS—JUST ADD SUNSHINE, OUR SEEDS WILL DO THE REST.

Kinsolving was at the sideboard, worrying the cork from the fresh bottle. This country would drive any man to a more or less steady routine of drinking, but it seemed to Cord that Kinsolving lived for the bottle.

"Sit down." Kinsolving poured the last of three drinks. "Grub will be ready in a few minutes." Cord took a chair with his back to the front door. From the kitchen came the odor of frying meat. Four plates, four glasses; the child Aggie had mentioned a woman, and there was that extra horse in the stable. So Kinsolving had a lady friend.

Cord let his whiskey sit. Kinsolving cleared his throat and did not say anything. Awkward discomfort was palpable in the room, though Chi seemed untouched by it, composed and relaxed. But Cord had some personal experience with bourbon whiskey, and he knew how it could push a man through changes. You could never keep up with the moods of some hard drinkers; it was like sharing a room with six different people, one of them always

coming on to you and you never knowing which one would
start in next.

So Cord expected to accomplish only the simple task of
finding out what Kinsolving had in mind. Later he could
figure out what to do about it. But one thing was certain:
The bond between them was long in the past. All that
remained was an unpaid debt.

Right then the door from the kitchen opened and a
woman backed through it, forks and spoons in one hand and
salt and pepper shakers in the other. She was tall, slim-
hipped, and small-breasted, her angular figure little softened by the white shirtwaist and apron over a straight black
skirt. Her dark hair was pinned up, the errant strands damp
from the cooking steam.

The woman's gaze was hard and somehow predatory, like
that of a gambler staring at poker hands and figuring odds.
What do you mean to me, her look said. *What is the
measure of your worth? Can I use you, or are you a threat?*
Her eyes were ebony-dark, and she held them on Cord as
she set the table, before glaring at Chi.

Over the years Chi had grown used to the idea of other
women excluding her from their notion of society. Women
looked on Chi with disapproval, suspicion, condemnation,
or fear. Even with envy, but never with friendship, never
with acceptance. That was all right though, long as they let
her be. Cord had a hunch this one would not.

He stood, and Kinsolving, taken by surprise, almost
knocked over his chair in following. "This here is Mae.
Miss Mae Cornell. These are Mister Cord and Miss Chi,
that I was telling you about, Mae."

Chi nodded. Cord said, "Hello," and got the same back,
along with a thin-lipped smile no warmer than the Kansas
gale. Mae's eyes were too small, or maybe set too close.

She looked to be in her twenties, about half Kinsolving's age.

Kinsolving put an arm around her waist, then took it quickly away, like he'd been caught at something improper. To occupy his hands, he picked up his glass. "Drink up, folks. We got something to celebrate."

"I'll have coffee," Chi said to Mae Cornell.

The thin woman's eyes went darker. Despite the apron and housewifely trappings, Cord had already figured out that Mae Cornell was not the sort to cook some man's meals and scrub his floors by day, and then lie passionlessly supine while he did his quick, rough business at night. Not and call that a life. So she would not like this game of serving maid, especially not for another woman—not one like Chi.

"Coffee sounds fine," Cord said, mildly as he could manage. Mae Cornell turned on her heel, returning from the kitchen with three cups and a tin pot. She set the cups at each place but Kinsolving's, so the older man reached across and grabbed Cord's glass and drained it, almost defiantly.

The meal was salty bacon and beans and stale hardtack. A man needed fresh meat to keep up his strength in weather like this, and it didn't look to Cord like he'd be seeing any in this Weed town. "There we go," Kinsolving said pointlessly when Mae set out the food, and after that no one spoke. Mae Cornell kept sneaking studying looks at Chi, but Chi seemed done with the woman and did not glance up.

Kinsolving pushed away his half-full plate and reached for the whiskey bottle. "What about her?" he said suddenly.

Cord's fork was halfway to his mouth. "How's that?"

Kinsolving inclined his head in Chi's direction. "I got things to say now, things that don't want to be nosed around. So we got to decide right here if she is in, because if so she has got to pull all the way."

Chi slapped her palm down on the table. "What about *her?*"

"Easy," Cord said. He pushed his own plate toward Kinsolving. "There is no question," he told the other man.

"Cord, we are talking serious money."

Chi snorted. "Speak your piece, hombre. Tell us the story we have come six hundred miles to hear."

"I don't think—" Mae Cornell began.

All Chi did was point a finger at the other woman, but it worked good as a slap across the face. Mae went a shade more pale, and Chi smiled a killer smile. "That's right," Chi said. "You don't think, and you stay quiet. Whatever happens in this town, I'll never have any need for you. I'll hurt you. Believe in that, *puta.*"

Mae Cornell opened and closed her mouth. Then her head whipped around and she turned her angry glare on Kinsolving. He licked his lips and said nothing. She stood, shaking with anger, and was turning away when she thought of how to save the situation for herself.

She looked down at Kinsolving and laughed.

There was loathing and derision and no humor in the sound, and it seemed to echo for a moment after she had shut the kitchen door behind her. Backed into a corner, this woman would bite the head off a snake, Cord figured. She had turned on the weakest person at the table with the coyote instincts of a carrion eater.

Kinsolving looked miserable, deflated. He drank his drink, and then he squared his shoulders with the resolve of a man about to dive into an icy creek.

"Most times," the old man said finally, "trains don't stop in Weed during the winter. They don't stop much any time, unless there is a boxcar of supplies for the merc, or some piece of special-order farming equipment from Saint Louis. In June and at the end of the summer there is flatcars for the wheat sacks, but that's only three or so weeks a year. Rest of the time the place is only a whistle-stop, when someone wants off."

"Sure," Chi said blandly, "but who would want off here?"

Kinsolving had been talking in a low, almost toneless voice, but now he spoke with a little heat. "Well now, miss, you might be surprised."

"Surprise me."

"There's people coming tomorrow, about midday. And we are going to be mightily glad to see them." Kinsolving poured and drank and wiped the corner of his mouth on the side of his wrist.

"One week ago," Kinsolving went on, "I was informed by telegraph about this train. It's going to be in the yard half an hour maybe, whatever it takes to lade on wood and water."

"Here in Weed," Cord said, half to himself.

"That's right. And not because the place is so pretty neither. The folks on this train, they don't want to be bothered by a crowd of people rubbernecking around. These are folks who like being left alone. Which is why I was informed, as the duly constituted law in Prine County. I was asked to assist in any way I could, make sure the townsfolk don't get in the way of orderly railroad business. They suggested it would not be a bad idea, either, if I had all my deputies in the near vicinity." Kinsolving barked a short laugh. "Good thing Tom got back when he did."

"Some kind of brass hat," Cord guessed. "A senator or a capitalist, or some other kind of heavyweight crook."

"Sure. A onetime claim-jumper named J. C. Arbuckle. Except now he is J. C. Arbuckle Minerals and Metals, out of New York City. Not that he is going to be personally riding that train."

Kinsolving grinned, warmed by his story and the whiskey. "This Arbuckle owns some paying mines in the high-mountain country north of Durango, around Silverton, Ouray, Telluride, those parts in Colorado. I don't have to tell you it isn't easy to get in there this time of winter, and this year has been especially contrary. It has been storming up there since October, and Arbuckle's people have not been able to deliver the Christmas payroll, which is now some six weeks overdue. The miners started out sullen, and now they have moved on to shooting-mad.

"Unless he pays them off quick," Kinsolving said, "the best thing Arbuckle can hope for is a strike that would shut him down until spring. The worst thing would be for the boys to start blowing dynamite in the deep shafts. Being a man who will spend a dollar to save ten, Arbuckle has chartered a train from New York to Denver and over the Divide, where there is a pack-train crew of hardy men waiting to carry in the payroll, plus late bonuses."

Kinsolving placed both hands on the table palms down. "There is two hundred thousand dollars on that train, give or take. We are going to take it, every goddamned penny."

"Just like that?" Chi asked.

"That's right."

"There'll be guards."

"I hope to shout. Pinkerton detectives, one dozen of them."

Mae Cornell was in the room again, standing with her back against the kitchen door. Cord had not seen her come easing through. "Three guns," Cord said to Kinsolving. "Three guns against a dozen at least."

"Four, with Bowen."

Cord wondered what to make of that. Maybe the moody young deputy was tied to Kinsolving in a way like Cord, or maybe he was just willing to take a foolish risk for big money. Lots of men were.

"I told him about it this morning," Kinsolving said. "He wants to come along."

"All right, four. Those are still long odds."

"Got to be." Kinsolving wrapped both hands around his whiskey glass. "You see, Mister Cord, you are the only one. Of all the boys in the old days, you were the one never went back on a man. You are here now: That proves it."

Mae Cornell would not take her eyes from Cord.

Chi said, "You tell me how we are going to do this thing."

"There is only one way to go, the way I see it," Kinsolving said. "When the train crew gets down to unload, the Pinkertons can do one of two things: Either they climb down to stretch their legs, or they sit tight. If they do the first, we take them, easy enough. If they stay put, we take the trainmen and then we wait. The Pinkertons are holed up in there without food or water to last, and that train is going nowhere. Sooner or later they will come out. In any case, we are sitting pretty."

"You are going to dry-gulch them," Chi said.

"Call it what you want."

"There are problems to it," Cord said. "Apart from the cold-blooded killing."

"Have your sensibilities gone too delicate, Mister Cord?" It was Mae Cornell. "Have you put aside killing for money in your older days?"

Cord was not sure which was stranger, her outburst or that Kinsolving did not shut her up. Chi shook her head in disgust.

"First," Cord said to Kinsolving, "those Pinkertons are generally men who know some things about guns and guarding and train robbers, and how to deal with them.

They do not figure to be quite so easy as you are saying."

Cord held up two fingers. "Second, Pinkerton detectives are a kind of lawman. Not official, but near enough to make it hard on anyone who goes up against them. Lawmen take it hard when one of their own is killed. They will let other things drop after a time, but not that. There would be heat on us for the rest of our lives, and none of us wants to take that on."

"Not even for two hundred thousand dollars?"

"That's right," Chi snapped.

Cord felt the same. Not only did Kinsolving make a damned poor partner, but there was plenty else to this he did not like. "But you sent for me before you knew anything about this payroll train."

"There's always one payroll or another." Kinsolving smiled like a judge. "Anyway, I had me a general idea."

Yes, you did, Cord thought, *a general idea to use me any way you could, if it got you some money and out of this damned place.* He was getting an inkling where the idea started—Mae Cornell. It pained Cord to see a man come to such a pass: too little nerve for his own dirty business, but the brass to ask someone else to do it for him.

There was an accusation in the hard gaze Chi was giving Cord: *You should have paid this one off long ago.* Sure, he knew that. When you failed to tidy up, the past came hunting you with bad news every time.

The faintest slur toward drunkenness had come into Kinsolving's voice. His face was doughier, his jowls red and too thick. He showed Cord a slack-jawed grin. "You are in, Cord. You know you are." He raised his glass. "Drink up."

"John P. . . ."

"Drink up, goddamn you." For a moment the sheriff sounded like the man he had been. "To old times, Cord, you and me."

Kinsolving drank and refilled his glass and drank again. Mae Cornell's smile was blank as a mummer's mask.

"Rest easy, folks," Kinsolving announced. "There is not a damned thing that can stand in our way."

Chi leaned toward him. "There's some hombres camped outside town," she said, "who might have themselves a different idea."

Chapter Seven

C HI SAT ON THE BARE MATTRESS ON THE IRON-framed bedsprings, watching Cord stack kindling in the fireplace in a cross-hatched square. He was absorbed in the task, as if the fire would not work unless immaculately built. When the kindling was blazing but still held its shape, Cord added a single chunk of split cordwood, waited a few moments, then added another before standing and dusting his hands together. The firemaking had taken the better part of a half hour, and in that time Chi had watched, unmoving.

Around the edge of the window, the wind blew needles of cold air into the room about the mercantile. On the floor of the wardrobe Cord found a scrap of something that might have been a union suit and tore it up for chinking. No one was abroad in the street; the town stood mute and still.

Presently the room began to warm. Cord shrugged out of his heavy leather coat and tossed it on the foot of Chi's bed. Arms draped over her knees, she was toying absently with the wide bracelet on her left wrist, Cord's gift, watching the play of firelight on the turquoise and silver.

Cord let himself drift, back to the afternoon in Juárez when they had exchanged gifts. In ten long years they had never been so right together, money in their britches and no lawmen nosing down their trail, no young boys with big guns and little sense gambling their lives for some power they thought Cord could pass to them with his death. And Cord had stayed off the bourbon whiskey and away from the dark places the drinking led him, always into various troubles and away from her.

They were careful to keep a firm line between themselves, so there was no confusion between respect and affection, between partnering and love. The rules were specific, if not so easily observed: Men and women were a natural business, but they could only keep each other sane until jealousy and the demands of one-on-one relationships took over. So for them there could be nothing named love, and surely no sex, if it were to stay clean. Cord had known his share of women and had cared for some more than he sometimes wished to recall, but he knew that no rules for love existed. For him and Chi the rule had to be, Cherish the companionship, and hands off. Anything else would betray them both.

Yet lately Cord had found himself wondering. Maybe, in another day, in another life on down the road . . .

But not now, not in this town of Weed. This was not a time for maundering thoughts of maybe. This was a time for figuring out how to stay alive through the coming showdown, for working through ways of dealing with the old sheriff half-crazed by whiskey and a lifetime of defeat, and his sharp-faced woman and his sullen deputy. For figuring the odds of holding off the ten rat-pack killers holed up in that sod-house on the snowy prairie. For thinking on train robbery, and a dozen or so hired Pinkerton guns.

A knot in one of the logs exploded and sparks spiraled up the chimney flue. Cord stared into the dancing firefly pattern and began to explain how this business had begun, twelve years before.

Cord had been in his early twenties, and not long beyond his drover's days. The time in question, he was one of seven men signed on by a road agent named O. N. Barnes, an easygoing man who was almost bald and missing two fingers on his left hand. It was early autumn, and in Red Bluff, California, the safe in the express company office would be full of wool money from the sheep ranches up in the coastal hills. The men Barnes had picked came together at a camp on Feather River, pretty lowland oak-tree country above the farms of the Sacramento Valley.

One of those men was John P. Kinsolving.

Even then, Kinsolving had some eight years of banditry behind him. In those days, before whiskey had softened his gut and muddled his self-notions, he was hard, self-confident, a man. Once he had run his own gang, but that ended when he drew time in the territorial prison in Yuma—more than a year before he busted out. Yuma was hard time, Kinsolving said, with bullwhips and worse, but he wasn't out of the game, not yet.

"I liked him in those days," Cord said, telling his story to Chi. "He was all right. But I didn't take to him right off, like you do with some people." *Like you,* Cord thought.

In that Feather River camp, while they waited out the wool sales, Kinsolving talked about changing ways. Whatever happened, men teamed up had to stick, he said. Partnering: There was the essence of it, a way of going past fear and loneliness with someone you could stake your life on. After a time Cord came to see Kinsolving was offering to partner with him. It was a possibility. Kinsolving struck Cord as capable, honest, and surely tough enough, and he was flattered by the proposition. Kinsolving had been down the trail, and still he saw Cord as worth his trouble.

But first there was the matter of the Red Bluff express office, and there is where things started to go wrong.

One of Barnes's bunch was a dandified grifter named Burton Elliott. Elliott's outlaw experience had more to do with confidence dodges than gunwork; he would have made a good professor selling miracle elixir from the back of a covered buckboard. This Elliott was the advance man for the Red Bluff job, spending time in town getting the feel of the layout of the express office, hanging around the saloons and barber shops and the lobby of the Tremont Hotel picking up what he could about the wool auctions and their proceeds.

Cord disliked the dapper conman from the git-go. He was always posing as someone else, as if he had played so many roles he had lost sight of himself. And he was a card cheat. That was lying to your partners in a way, although Cord, no gambler himself, figured men who were too dumb to know they were being fleeced deserved what they got.

"I was an arrogant pup," Cord said to Chi.

She smiled. "Worse than now?"

"That's right," Cord said. "Lots worse."

The way it turned out, Burton Elliott was more than a four-flusher and a fake: On one of his scouting trips he betrayed the whole bunch to the Wool Growers' Protective Association, and the law.

The bunch broke camp on the Feather River and rode downstream for Red Bluff on a bright, vibrant fall day. They drifted through rolling dry-grass hills and oak trees clustered along the ridges as if nothing could ever touch them with harm, not in a life where the air smelled so perfectly clean and the horses did not lather under the bluebird sky.

They drifted into Red Bluff from different directions, singly or in pairs over a period of a half hour, acting casual, anticipating success. With his cut Cord was going to ride south for the winter, find himself a woman whose company and conversation he could abide, and spend his days drinking in the sunshine and his nights making comfortable, unhurried love. He had gotten it into his head that Florida was the place to go.

"Florida!" Chi was amused.

"Well, I never did get there."

"Jesus, Cord." She shook her head. "Some of the ideas you have."

Cord and Kinsolving, the outside men, rode into Red Bluff last. The clock below the dome on the Tehama County Courthouse wore gilt Roman numerals that flashed in the low autumn sunlight. It was one minute before three.

O. N. Barnes and another man came out of a saloon called the Union Station and started across the street to the express office. Their horses were already hitched in front along with the other four men's animals. Another pair came down the boardwalk, and a fifth was nearing from the other direction. Burton Elliott was last to show.

As the six men began filing into the office, Cord bent in the saddle and gathered up the bridle reins of three horses. Kinsolving got hold of the other three.

Burton Elliott, bringing up the rear, stopped suddenly and pulled the door shut behind the other five. He headed off down the boardwalk, walking quickly.

A splintered second after that signal, a terrific volley of gunfire exploded inside the office.

The front windows shattered. One of the horses Cord

held snorted and reared, and fell heavily. Others jerked loose and scattered in a bolt down the street.

Everything was haywire, and Cord was lost like a child in the confusion. It was a lesson never forgotten: Figure everything can go wrong, and you will never be surprised. To survive you must stay ahead of the chaos—and there will be chaos.

But Kinsolving knew instantly. "Elliott!" he barked.

The dandified conman should have run, but for some dumb reason he had held up to watch. He wheeled away when Kinsolving called his name.

"You cold-deck-dealing son of a bitch," Kinsolving spat, and he shot Elliott in the back.

Men with rifles appeared on rooftops.

Cord put spurs to his horse as lead began to kick up dust all around him. Cord knew he was going to die.

The bullet took him in the side. He felt the shock of impact, as if someone had punched him, just above his belt and to the right of his spine. Kinsolving was at his side and they were racing out of town at a dead low run, hooves drumming on the dried hardpan roadway.

Then the pain came, unlike anything Cord had ever felt, and sudden, going from discomfort to agony in a few heartbeats. White-hot metal was buried deep in his guts, searing flames consumed all of his insides. He could smell his flesh burning. The trail down by the river dimmed then disappeared as he went blind, and he could not scream. Dying carried more terror than he could have imagined.

Cord fell, but he did not strike the ground. In one last lucid flash he felt new pain stabbing into his belly. Later he understood that it had been Kinsolving's saddle horn.

The fear: that part Cord never forgot. Knowing it that intimately, another man might have lost his nerve afterward, but Cord was fortunate: As he saw it, he had experienced the unbearable and come back, had borne it and knew some of its mystery. He had found the wolf in his heart.

"I should have died," Cord told Chi. He was standing at the window of her room, seeing his story in the gray texture of the snowstorm outside. He shivered as a cold draft licked at his neck. "I came close. I don't recall a thing for a week, but I guess I came to a couple of times, enough to rave and drink from a canteen. When I returned to the world, Kinsolving was sitting over me where I was laid out on the ground. We were in the high country north of Lassen Peak. It was cool but I was sopping in my sweat—you could have wrung a gallon from my union suit. When I tried sitting up it was like my guts were ripping loose, and I passed out again. You ever been shot?"

"Yes," Chi said.

Cord was surprised, and lost the thread of his story for a moment. It had to have happened in the years before they formed their team against the world, during the time they did not talk about. He was curious but did not ask. The past was another country.

"Finish your tale, Cord," Chi said gently.

"I should have died," Cord said again, "but I didn't. That Winchester forty-four slug went almost the whole way through me, so Kinsolving could feel the lump under my skin, down in my groin. He cut me open with his Buck knife and pulled it out with his fingers, all slippery with blood. Then he broke open cartridges and poured black powder over both wounds and set it afire to cauterize them. Even so there was green pus oozing out, and I was burning with fever and crazed as a mustang. But none of it killed me, which is the virtue of being young. Three months passed before I could go more than a half hour without the need to pass water. But then it eased off and I was well, and none of it ever bothered me again." With this last, his tone was almost defiant.

"Except for Kinsolving."

"Right." Cord calmed himself. "I never asked him for particulars of how he got us away, and he never volunteered, except to laugh about swimming the Sacramento with me slung across like a sack of sugar. I got the idea men were shot in the getaway, maybe lawmen among them, special deputies sworn in for the occasion of bushwacking us. He was hit himself, in the left elbow. The shot cracked the bone and it never was set right, which is why he's still got that peculiar twist to the arm. Lucky for him it wasn't his gun arm."

"Lucky for you too."

"There you are," Cord said. "I owe him my life."

He fetched another chunk from the split wood he had stacked in the corner. There was a fair-sized pile of glowing embers by now, so the cured wood burst into flame almost immediately.

"Here is how it ended," Cord said, talking to the fire. "We rode together another six months, through until the next spring. When I was well enough to move on, we skirted up through Redding and followed the Trinity down to the coast. We took a trading post on the Pacific Road north of Eureka just after the New Year. Then we went south out of the rain, and not long after we said our so-longs.

"There was something about Kinsolving," Cord went on, "that stuck in my craw. For a long time I could not put a name on it, so I thought it was just me and felt bad about it. But it was strong enough to get me split from him."

Cord looked over his shoulder at Chi sitting on her bed. "You know when it came to me?"

She shook her head.

"Five years back. That time we were in Santa Fe and that

tent show came through town. There was a Punch-and-Judy show—you were wandered off somewhere—about this German magic-man who sold his soul to the devil, that's where he got his powers. Maybe that sounds crazy, getting your answers from a Punch-and-Judy show, but out of nowhere I thought of Kinsolving. He had bought a piece of my soul. So I split from him."

"My good luck," Chi said.

Cord let that sink in. "I should have settled up first, but I was young and in a hurry. But there it always was: He was holding my paper, and someday he was going to call it in."

"Here we are."

"You see how it is."

A blast of wind hit the window hard enough to rattle glass. A scrap of the torn union suit fell to the floor and skittered across the room in front of a chill draft. Chi got up and stuffed the crack again.

"In that Punch-and-Judy," she said, "what happens to the German *brujo?*"

"He conjures up a special magic trick," Cord said. "The devil doesn't get his soul after all."

"Keep that in mind," Chi said, "when the shooting starts."

Chapter Eight

"LOOK THERE," CORD SAID.

Chi came over and stood beside him at the window. The ragamuffin child, Aggie, was standing in the middle of the street directly below, staring off south, the direction they had come in, out toward the prairie wash where Con James and his bunch were camped. Aggie's hair was dusted with snow, and the wind whipped clotted strands across her face.

Chi threw open the window, and Cord heard a low, inarticulate moaning sound that he had to strain to distinguish from the constant rush of storm.

"Muchacha," Chi called down.

Aggie gave no sign she heard. Chi called again, more loudly, using the child's name. Still Aggie did not look up. She stood rigid as a monument while the storm sifted silvery all around her.

Chi shut the window. She drew her Colt, removed one of the cartridges, and used her teeth to pull the slug from the casing before dumping the black powder into her palm. It was dry and friable, and flowed cleanly across her hand. Chi refilled the empty cylinder with a fresh cartridge from her belt and went out of the room.

A moment later she came out and went to the bedraggled girl and put her arm around the girl's thin shoulders. Chi bent her head to the girl's ear, and finally Aggie looked up to the dark gunwoman, as if only then had she become aware of her presence. Aggie shook her head no. Chi spoke again, and used both hands to turn her gently but firmly. The girl moved like a somnambulist, so Chi had to steer her. Cord watched until they moved inside the livery barn.

Cord built a smoke. It was lopsided and too fat in the middle, but it would serve. From the fireplace he took a stick of kindling and used it to light up. When he got back to the window, Kinsolving was leaving his office. The sheriff looked up to Cord through the slanting lines of snow and touched two fingers to the brim of his hat.

This had been a strange reunion so far. Kinsolving was too much changed; age and whiskey had cost him his understanding of the ways a man should act. And Kinsolving knew it, and resented Cord for being the witness to his shame. Cord was the man Kinsolving might have been. They were past being equals, and all that was left was the awkwardness and the uncomfortable silences.

But awkward was one thing, and dead was another. The train tomorrow: Where was the sense to that business? Cord had postponed such considerations, and felt angry at himself and at Kinsolving. Something had to be worked out in the next few hours.

Kinsolving came from the front room of the mercantile holding another bottle of whiskey by the neck. He walked into the wind with his head down and did not look up at Cord again before entering his office.

Then, his eyes now adjusted to the dim stormy light, Cord made out the figure of Mae Cornell. She wore a heavy cloth coat that reached to her ankles, and a red woolen scarf around her head and tied under her chin. She might have been there for some time.

After Kinsolving went inside, Mae Cornell sidled back toward the cabin at the office's rear. But then she reappeared on the other side, went down through the drifts to enter the livery by the side door. As Cord finished his smoke, one of the main double doors swung open and Mae came out, leading one of the sorry-looking geldings. She climbed up astride, her skirt riding above her shoe-tops to reveal the gray fringes of long underwear around the tops of her stockings. She pushed the door shut from the saddle and rode out, circling north around the livery before taking the trace out of town south.

When Chi led her mare from the barn a few moments later Cord was not surprised. She mounted, sitting erect against the storm. When she came abreast of the merc she looked to Cord and held up one thumb, then pointed a forefinger south. Cord had the urge to throw the window open and call down to her, but there was nothing to say. So he waved back and watched her ride out, and then she was gone in the storm like Mae Cornell.

Chapter Nine

DOWNSTAIRS IN THE WHISKEY ROOM, THE cast-iron belly-door of the stove was too hot for Cord's bare hand. He found a rag behind the bar and used it to wrestle the door open and add a couple of chunks atop the glowing embers. In the big back room he found a tin of coal oil, a glazed tin coffeepot, and a hand-crank grinder on the counter above the glass case. Cord went about his chores with precision and no thought at all.

He ground coffee and threw a half handful into the pot. Out back he had to drop the well-bucket twice before it broke the cap of ice that had formed since the last time someone drew water. He took the bucket inside, filled the coffeepot and set it on the stove, then filled the lamp from the tin of kerosene and trimmed and lit the wick. The brewing coffee began to hiss.

Cord looked around the barren room and, satisfied he had brought some order to it, went behind the bar. He found a bottle of what looked like bourbon, though there was no label. No doubt it had been called bourbon by the hapless mercantilist, even if it had been distilled well west of the Mississippi, and owed its flavor more to hickory sawdust and a soak of tobacco than any family secrets of distillery. Pouring a shotglassful, Cord took a deep breath and tossed it back. He was contemplating another, staring at the bottle and considering how badly he needed to drink, when Tom Bowen came in.

Bowen took off his Stetson and slapped it against his thigh. Snow fluttered to the floor and melted into little damp pinpoints. "That coffee smells all right," he said.

"Yeah," Cord said. "More than you can say for this whiskey."

Bowen's hard face came loose a little—not quite a grin, but near the idea. He went into the back room and returned with a couple of coffee cups and another whiskey bottle. This one had a printed label, and below the lithography the signature *James B. Beam*.

"I don't drink so much anymore," Bowen said, "but when I do . . ." He poured two cups of coffee, using the rag around the pot handle. "On my fourteenth birthday," he said, "my father allowed me one shot of bourbon. He said I should get the taste fixed in my mind and never forget. Then, if I had to drink, it would be good whiskey or nothing, and I would not go blind with poison. You could say such things in Kentucky, ten years back. They understood whiskey." All this came in a toneless voice flavored with a drawl subtle as the liquor's bite. Bowen sat one of the coffee cups before Cord.

Cord threw the shotglass load of rotgut into the stove, refilled from Bowen's bottle, and upended the glass into his coffee. After an exploratory sip, he nodded his satisfaction.

"Sanderson ordered it for me special," Bowen said, "before he run out on the country." He stood at the end of the plank bar, elbows on either side of his coffee cup. Cord moved the bottle a little toward him, but Bowen shook his head no.

They drank without speaking. Behind them the front window rattled like a spirit's bag of bones, and the firewood crackled counterpoint. Then Cord heard another sound, the mouselike scratching of tiny claws on the brittle frozen glass, and when he turned, Aggie's haggard face was framed between the mullions.

She opened her mouth in a long, mournful O, but when Cord took a step toward her she vanished, suddenly and absolutely as a burst balloon. Cord threw open the door and took a blast of wind-driven snow in the face. He went out on the boardwalk, but there was no sign of the girl.

"Her people were Yankees," Bowen said. Cord came back in and shut the door. "From eastern Pennsylvania, near Wilkes-Barre is what I heard. They were among the first to come into Prine County, not long after the war. There was no town and no railroad, hardly any other family folk, but there were nightriders, driven out here from the eastern part of the state."

Cord knew of the nightriders. During the war most of

them had been irregulars allied with the Army of the Confederacy, riding the Border States and bringing guerrilla tactics to bear against far outposts of the Union army. Their leaders were men like Bloody Bill Anderson and William Clarke Quantrill, and when the war was over and lost they were declared outlaw. Given the names, some of them embraced the act; among those were the nightriders. Cord had no truck for them: Terrorizing folk under cover of darkness and mob anonymity was his idea of pure chicken-livered nastiness.

"They killed off her people," Bowen said, "but first they used her mother while she watched. They let her be, because they thought she was too young to bear witness. God will judge them. Anyway, she hasn't been right since."

Cord was silent a moment. "Goddamn," he said, "there are things I cannot countenance. I wish one of those nightriding sons of bitches would come to play with me."

"She is frightened around men," Bowen said, "but it is guns that really send her into panic. I saw her with your partner."

"Those nightriders," Cord said. "Were you there?"

Bowen gave him a sharp look. "No. But there was a time I was not so different."

Cord had already sensed some darkness in Bowen's past, and wondered if it had something to do with Bowen's grudging loyalty to Kinsolving.

"She makes out." Bowen sipped at his coffee. "The girl, I mean. In the winter she stays in the livery, and in the summer she does chores out on the farms. She works hard enough, I hear, but she tends to get on people's nerves, all the time talking about the future and what's going to happen, and bad times always on the way."

"You are the county law."

"There is that, Mister Cord," Bowen said evenly. "Maybe you could say me or Kinsolving should see to her. Or maybe you could take her on, sort of adopt her, when you ride out. But then, she ain't that easy to get next to."

Bowen fetched the pot and refilled both cups. "Besides, people around these towns like Weed have got enough of their own troubles to deal on. Maybe you noticed."

"I'm the same. No orphans allowed."

"But you know troubles. Like right now, you are tucked into bed and snug up to Kinsolving's problems."

"And there," Cord said, "is what we are talking about."

Instead of answering, Bowen watched Cord dig out his makings and roll a smoke. But when Cord licked at the brown paper, it tore down the side. Bowen watched him strip the tobacco into his pouch, draw another paper, and begin over again. He seemed so interested in the process, Cord thought he was going to pipe up with suggestions.

But instead Bowen looked away and said, "When this all got started, I had a hunch what was driving the old man. I knew who you were soon as he named you, what you looked like too, seeing as how the Department of Justice would send us your picture every once in a while. I guess now that there's no more Federal paper on you, we won't be getting them posters. Too bad."

"Tell your story."

"Kinsolving figured to pull something outside the law and rope you in on it. There was lots I didn't like about the idea—still don't—but maybe it was just a pipe dream, or I wouldn't find you, or you wouldn't come back if I did.

"But then it came together," Bowen said, "as it will sometimes. Us arriving just when we did, day before the train, and all of a sudden the pipe dream turns real."

"Maybe."

"It's anyway a real possibility. Even if he is making a dead-man mistake."

"Such as?"

Bowen considered. "Let's say I don't want him killed, or living out his days behind penitentiary bars."

This smoke was better than Cord's first. He struck a lucifer under the bar. "You didn't tell him about Con James, waiting out there to take his train away. Why not?"

"Would that stop him?"

The deputy was right. Some ways he knew the old man better than Cord. Earlier that day, after the strained luncheon in Kinsolving's cabin, Chi had gone on to tell the sheriff about the ten men in the soddy. "Let 'em ride in," Kinsolving had said. "They won't amount to much. They will run into guns, and when that's over we'll see to the train."

Where had Kinsolving invented such grand conceits? Cord had once learned a lesson about vulnerability and humility from an old and courtly gunfighter named J. W. Baron: You could be fastest in the West, but you were still only a man with a gun. One bullet, a lucky shot, fired at your back from ambush—and you were dead meat. But in his mind Kinsolving had invested Cord with arcane powers, the antipode of his own defeats. That kind of unbridled imagining got men killed.

"Then there is the woman," Bowen said.

Mae Cornell was skulking all around the edges of this business, carrying Kinsolving's supper and all the marks of petty meanness as well. How far had she gone in pushing Kinsolving toward chasing this bad dream?

"I've been outside the law," Bowen said. "I didn't do so good, and I would have done worse if not for him. So I owe him too. I wasn't much of a bandit the first time, but I'll try it again if that's what he wants."

Bowen gestured for the bottle, and when Cord passed it Bowen splashed a dollop into his coffee. "We could ride away, you and me and your partner—would if we had any sense. But he'd just try it alone, go up against Con James and those Pinkertons and maybe Mae Cornell too, and he'd die."

"What do you have in mind?" Cord said.

"Stop him."

"You stop him."

"I can't."

"I can," Cord said. "But I won't."

"Why not?"

It was a good question, to which Cord had no good answer. There was the debt—but these days he was coming to see that his kind of rigid thinking could be a box canyon for the brain. It could kill you.

But so could too much rationalization. When a fight was made and a man drew on you, you did not worry about anyone's immortal soul, because you had decided that one long before: Never flinch, shoot to kill.

"What I do doesn't tie you in," Cord said. "You just think on this: You get involved in taking that train, and you are into a lifetime of running, and men tracking you down to kill you because you are worth money. Your carcass, anyway." Cord took back the bottle. "Do you owe him all that?"

"Do you?"

Cord flung his cigarette butt against the wall and pointed a finger at Bowen. "You watch your goddamned mouth, boy," he said, his voice icy as the wind. He hated the notion of Bowen seeing through him like window glass.

"He didn't ask."

Cord blinked. "How's that?"

"Kinsolving didn't ask me to take a hand. Fact is, he told me to ride out. I wouldn't."

"Shit." Cord was disgusted with every part of this. He filled his glass and did not pour it into his coffee but downed it neat.

Behind him the door banged open and Chi came in, glancing first at Cord's glass, and then at the bottle, four fingers down. She frowned slightly, said, "*Hola,*" and went to the stove. Her cheeks were deep crimson, and snow had plastered against the windward side of her leather saddle-britches.

"Snow is picking up," she said, flexing her fingers over the stove's heat.

"Maybe there won't be any railroad train," Bowen said.

"There will be. Depend on it." Chi went behind the bar and searched out what looked to be a bottle of tequila. She sat it on the planks while she poured herself coffee. She downed a shot of the clear liquor, then sipped at the hot brew. "There are things happening that nobody has figured on."

"All the damn time," Cord said, still in his mad.

Chi gave him a narrow look. "That woman—Kinsolving's *puta*—she rode out, couple of hours back."

"Wildcat weather for traveling," Cord muttered.

"*Loco.*"

Cord nodded toward Bowen. "He's in too. We are all *loco.*"

"She rode out to that soddy," Chi said.

"And rode right in." Bowen straightened. "Like her and those boys are old friends."

"Which they are," Chi said.

Cord swore. It fit in with what he'd seen of the woman—and so what? If he went to Kinsolving and told him the bitch was all trick and no substance, it would stop nothing. Cord saw the future laid out like a map with only one road.

"What about us, Cord?" Chi broke into his thoughts. "We've got all the puzzle pieces now. What do we make of them? We got some hard talk coming, you and me."

The room was too warm. Chi's long braids were wet with melted snow.

"*Mañana*," Chi pressed. "What do we do?"

Cord shook his head. He did not like being treed, but he had no good answer for Chi.

Chapter Ten

CORD USED HIS THIN-BLADED STOCKMAN'S knife to pry open a tin of boiled meat. It smelled slightly rancid, but he didn't suppose it would kill any of them. He needed meat, even if he had to settle for this green-brown variety. He dumped the tin into a saucepan, opened and added another, and splashed water from the bucket over it all. He sat the pan atop the stove and punched up the fire.

Then Cord filled a larger kettle and set it to boil. He peeled four half-frozen potatoes he'd found in the root cellar beneath the trapdoor in the back room, paring away the black and green spots until there wasn't much left. He tossed them in the kettle when the water began to bubble. Then he dumped out the coffeepot in the slop bucket behind the bar and put on fresh. He worked mechanically, mindlessly; he'd been sipping along steadily at Tom Bowen's bourbon.

Chi sat at the round table sipping tequila. Beside her was the girl Aggie, preoccupied by the tattered deck of cards, turning them one by one. Each time she came to a picture card she squealed with delight.

Here is a pretty domestic scene of folks at their supper, Cord thought. *Delicious fresh grub on the way, along with fine grown-up conversation and all the other trappings of gracious living on the Great Plains of America. Who could ask for more?*

Aggie held up the king of spades and chirped, "Look, the black king. Do you know the black king? Is it him?" She was gesturing at Cord.

He scowled, and her grin of careless idiocy slackened. Chi touched the girl reassuringly on the shoulder and shot Cord a reproachful look. "Tough man."

"Is he the black king?" Aggie asked in a small voice.

"No, *niña.*"

"I knew he wasn't." Aggie ruffled through the deck and began to pick out all the spades. "The black king is out there, with all the other black men." She began to lay out the spades in numerical order, counting out loud, deuce through ten. "Nine black men, and the black king," she announced, and laid out an eleventh card. "There is the black queen. I know them all."

"Hush, *muchacha.*"

The girl bunched the cards into a jumbled pile. "Now we can't see the black men. They are hiding."

"That's right, *chica.*"

"But they can see us."

"Jesus Christ," Cord exploded. "Will you for God's sake make her stop?"

Chi's voice was cold. "If you don't like it, get out."

"Not before my supper," Cord said, sounding like a child himself.

But a few minutes later, after Cord laid out plates and poured hot coffee and set the two pans of food on the table, Chi took a bite and said, "You are a lucky man, Mister Cord."

"How's that?"

"You shoot better than you cook. Otherwise you would be years dead."

She was always quick to anger but could not hold it, while Cord steamed and did not forget. Once it was finished, this business with Kinsolving would never be brought to her mind, except as a good story. Cord would rankle over it for months.

The potatoes were mushy on the outside and starchy within, and the canned beef was stringy as jerked bison and gritty with salt, but it was hot and there was plenty of it. You had to have meat to keep a body together in this weather, even though Cord hated tinned food. "Better than bacon and beans," he said. They'd been asked to Kinsolving's cabin for this meal, but neither had the appetite for that.

Aggie ate with total concentration, gnawing off a bite of meat, chewing thoughtfully, and swallowing before taking another. Chi leaned close and whispered in her ear, and Cord was irritated. What could come of Chi's attachment to the child? Did she think they would take her along when they left this goddamned town? Here was another path to trouble to worry about.

Then the door rattled and trouble walked right in.

Reuben C. Greyson still stank. He stood in the open doorway with the wind blowing in around him, until Chi snapped, "Shut the door, *cabrón.*"

Cord watched the expressions parade across Greyson's thick black-bearded features, and he read in them all that had happened to the dull-witted bully since he'd been humiliated by Chi the night before. He saw Greyson waking up hurting but close to his old self in the morning, full-up with hatred. Chi had jabbed him in the balls and Cord had kicked in a rib and he had been made a fool again. The physical hurts would not be serious; men like Reuben Greyson were too coarse-sensed for the subtleties of pain. But the contempt those other nine men would have been pouring on him all day would be hard to endure. A woman had mortified him. They would call him a girl and a sheep and a boy and worse, and then laugh. Greyson would try drinking; "brave-up" was what some men called whiskey, but it would not help Greyson because he would know there was no revenge in facing Chi in a straight shoot-down. So he would drink some more and think about other ways, like back-shooting. Now he was here.

Greyson licked his sausage lips and slammed the door.

"They sent me in," Greyson said. "Con and them, they sent me in for more whiskey. If anything happens, if I don't come back, they'll miss me."

"No, they won't," Chi said. "Nobody ever missed you."

Aggie's face was pale as the snow. Chi petted her hair and the girl did not bolt, but looked like any moment she might.

Behind the bar Greyson stuffed a bottle in either pocket of his greasy buckskin jacket and took another by the neck. He was doing nothing for Cord's sour mood, but trouble in front of the girl would not help. Greyson was still behind the bar, his brows furrowed, as if he were trying to think something through and having a hell of a time of it. Then he came around and over to the table.

"Let's have us a drink," he said.

Cord and Chi kept silent. This meaningless baiting over who drinks with whom, or Chi's fine looks—they had stopped reacting to that nonsense years ago. Gunplay was pure: a matter of pain and living and dying.

"Yeah," Greyson said. "We will have us a drink." He hooked a chair with his foot and lowered his bulk into it. With his teeth he pulled the cork and took a long gurgling pull before setting the bottle in front of Chi. "What say, lady? Let's drink to bygones be bygones."

"Cord," Chi said, in a pleasant conversational tone, "you ever count the funny reasons people get killed?"

Greyson lost a shade of bully-bluster. "What're you saying?"

"You've had your drink. Get out of here."

"You listen to the lady," Cord said. "You remember last night. This time she will shoot. Try her."

"Get out," Chi said again.

Greyson pushed back his chair. "I'll be here tomorrow," he said, "and I won't be alone." He spat on the floor. "I'll walk in your blood."

Chi's serape swept back and there was her Colt, maybe a foot from Greyson's fat gut. His feet got tangled with the chair as he tried to stand, and he went down with a crash of shattering glass. Whiskey from the broken bottle made a puddle beneath him.

Chi was on her feet. Holding her Peacemaker steady, she took up the open bottle and smashed it on the floor a few inches from Greyson's head. He cowered and scuttled back, walking on his elbows.

"You won't see any blood but your own," Chi rasped. "The killing starts right now. I am going to shoot me a pig."

Aggie screamed and leaped from her chair, and Chi's eyes left Greyson. Cord did not wait to see what Greyson would try in that moment. He threw the table forward, dishes and cups and pans flying down on Greyson. The heavy kettle *thwunk*ed into his head. Cord kicked the table clear as he drew.

The kettle had opened a cut at Greyson's hairline; blood was streaming over his forehead and into one eye. Greyson ignored it; it took all his minimal concentration to stand. Cord had the door open. Greyson went through it like a drunk, bouncing off both sides of the jamb. Cord threw it shut behind him.

He watched from the window. Greyson got himself erect and made his horse. Cord kept his eye on him until he was mounted and lost in the snow-streak. It was full dark now.

The door leading back to the mercantile was open, and when Cord passed through he saw the door to the outside was ajar as well. He closed them both.

"She's gone," he said. Chi pulled the table upright and set the chairs back around it. Cord pulled out his gold watch. Almost six o'clock.

Then Aggie screamed, a far-off howl of terror.

Chi was out the door first, but Cord was fast after her. The livery was a vague dark hulk beyond the sheeting snow. Chi yanked the door open as Cord came up.

Aggie screamed again, her tone so anguished that Cord felt chilled, the more so because he had not thought any screaming could ever frighten him again. Inside, his bay gelding reared against his hitch, pawing his forehooves at the boards of his stall. A lantern glowed diffusely from the last partition.

A hand slapped flesh and Greyson grunted, "You shut up, little girlie."

Chi drew as Cord moved past her, shuffling silently along the dirt-floor aisle between stalls, his boots pushing through scattered hay.

Greyson was in the last stall, snorting and rutting, Aggie almost hidden under the mass of his gross shape.

Anger had been eating at Cord all afternoon, and he lost himself. He pulled Greyson off by the face, fingers groping for eyesockets. Cord got a fleeting glance of Aggie's bony body, her skirt rucked up around her waist, a bright smear of blood between her legs and across her face, before she rolled clear of the lamplight. Greyson grappled for Cord's wrists, and Cord slammed him against the stall.

Greyson gasped and came up, apelike, arms hanging down and his hammy fists balled. The cut on his forehead oozed blood, but he did not seem to notice.

Cord punched him in the middle of the face, throwing so much of his weight behind it he finished on one knee. Greyson hit the back wall and slipped to the floor. His nose was broken and adding to the blood all over his face, but Greyson was smiling. Here was the sort of trouble he had been seeking all along.

He drew his feet under him and charged Cord like a bull, head down. Cord sidestepped, but Greyson's shoulder caught him in the lower ribs and Cord heard something crack as the momentum carried him off his feet. Greyson's knee gouged at Cord's groin but glanced off his thigh instead. The big man's hands grabbed for Cord's eyes. But he was blinded by the blood washing down his face.

Cord clasped his hands together in a double fist. He brought it down on the back of Greyson's neck with all his strength. Greyson howled in Cord's face, spitting blood, but then his bulk was no longer pressing Cord into the dirty straw.

Cord rolled clear and made his feet, breathing hard. Greyson retreated into the stall, dropped his shoulder, and made ready for anoher charge.

"*Puerco!*" Chi screamed. "Look at me!"

Greyson shook his head dully and wiped blood from his eyes with his buckskin sleeve.

"Look at me, pig bastard!"

Greyson looked up into terror.

Right behind Cord a gun went off.

Greyson lifted off his feet and punched back into the stall. A geysering spurt of blood pumped from a hole high up on his chest, and his body convulsed and was still.

Cord stared down. Greyson's .45 was in his holster, his hand nowhere near the gun.

Cord turned and looked incredulously at Chi.

Her left arm was around the sobbing girl; with her right, she holstered the smoking Colt. Her face was ugly with rage, so it was Cord who looked away, confused and even frightened. There was wetness on his cheek. He swiped at it and saw on his hand a ropy strand of Greyson's bloody spittle.

"What he did, Cord, had nothing to do with the *niña*." Chi's voice shook. "The pig *cabrón* had to hurt someone, and he could not hurt you or me. She was all he could manage." She looked to where the blood was seeping away into the manure around Greyson's cooling body. "I killed him too fast. I'd've liked to walk around in him with boots on, so he had plenty of time to think."

Aggie gasped into Chi's serape, sobbing the same animal mewling sounds Cord had heard her make in the street. Chi spun the girl and held her in place, pointing her toward the spread-eagled corpse.

"Look at him, *hija*," Chi insisted, almost cruelly. "Look and see. He is dead. He is dead and you are alive, and he will never hurt you again."

The girl stared, still as wood. The blood on her face had mostly wiped off on Chi's serape, so Cord saw it had come from Greyson's cut. He wondered if the dead man had even been capable of the act he tried to force on the girl.

"He is dead and gone to the devil," Chi hissed. She shook the girl by the shoulders.

Aggie screamed and twisted away hard enough to break Chi's grip. Chi let her go. They could hear her muffled sobs from somewhere at the other end of the livery. Chi glared at Cord and went to the girl.

Cord's hands were trembling. The fight should have leeched some of the anger, but instead he was worse, resentful and bewildered, and alone in this shit-smelling stable. He remembered the crack when Greyson butted him, and took a deep cautious breath, but no ribs stabbed into places they should not. He stretched, and was all right.

But then he fished in his vest pocket. The gold cover of the Hamilton was dented, and the latch would not open it. Cord used his knife. When he pried the case apart, watchworks dribbled out into the straw.

Away in the livery stable, Chi was crooning a soft Spanish singsong. The girl was still weeping. Cord listened and stared into the watch case, rereading Chi's inscription in the sooty faltering lamplight.

Chapter Eleven

S OON AS CORD STEPPED BACK INTO THE
liquor room, he saw trouble was gathering a head of
steam. That was fine. The only watch he'd ever owned was
ruined, and he was in the mood to clean house.

Con James sat at the round table. A dark cup of coffee
was before him, and he was polishing his round-lensed
spectacles with a dirty checked bandana. His rough-out
leather coat hung over a chair near the stove, giving off a
dank, musty odor as it began to steam.

Cord went past the table as if it were unoccupied. On the
backbar shelf he found a cloudy-sided shotglass and filled it
with Jim Beam, right to the brim, and drank it off. But the
smell of Reuben Greyson's stinking breath was still in his
nostrils, and it colored everything, even the whiskey's taste.
Cord poured and drank again, and this time the Beam tasted
as it should, smoky and full of power.

"Somebody shot?" Con James inquired politely, like he
was asking after the health of Cord's kin.

"That's right." Cord's voice was raspy, as if the whiskey
had seared his throat.

"Damn that Greyson." James shook his head like an
indulgent father. He smiled at Cord. "Bet it was the woman.
He asked her for it, and damn me if she didn't look up to the
task."

"She always is," Cord said. "Keep that in mind."

James laughed. "Never forget it." He turned his grin on the man sitting next to him, a slick looker who was drinking nothing. He kept his hands on the table, palms down and side by side, as if he were vain about the taper of his long fingers. He had hair the color and texture of a thatched roof, tufts of it sticking out under the felt brim of his hard-used Stetson. One of his cheeks was freckled by a constellation of puckery little scars, each no bigger than the nail on a little toe. The rest of the cheek was peppered with dark specks. Somewhere down the line he had taken a load of buckshot in the face; the specks were unburned black powder, embedded under the skin like a tattoo.

"The boys were low on red-eye," James said, "and tending toward fractiousness. Reuben volunteered, and I gave him the go-ahead, but then I got to thinking. Maybe he had other things in mind besides whiskey-fetching. It worried me something terrible."

"But not about Greyson," Cord said.

"About the whiskey. Them boys would be highly disappointed at no drinks. Me being the leader, it was my job to see to it."

"Good work," Cord said.

James held up his polished spectacles toward the lamp, examined his work critically, then replaced them on his nose. He blinked at Cord. "There was a reason me and Coy here waited on you." Coy's eyes never left Cord.

Cord drank half his third shot of whiskey. The smooth warmth seeped down his gullet into the deepness of his gut, then crawled back up his spine into his head. He was starting to feel all right. One or two more, figuring on his past experience with Jim Beam, and he would feel good and mean.

"I'll give you a fair chance," James said.

"That so."

"After you-all rode on this morning, some of the boys—Jasey Crook, Mac Cobb, the nigger, Reuben too, God take his soul—some of them recalled who you and the woman were. And I sure as hell knew the names of Cord and Chi. I've heard the tales."

James sipped at his cup and shook his head, as if the coffee were so good it was regretful. "Damned thoughtful tales they are, which is why I flat out do not want any sort of face-up with you or your partner. None one on one, anyway.

"But it's not a question," James went on. "Tomorrow when I come in there will be nine men backing my play—well, eight, now that Greyson is greased. That should be enough though; I made allowances when I planned it out. But understand: We are going to take that train, and if needs be we will kill you and your lady and whoever. It will happen, if you make it go that way."

Cord finished the third shot. "What about Mister Coy here? What does he do besides look mean? You going to stare me to death, Coy?" That kind of needling was pointless. It was the whiskey popping out—and the hell with it, Cord thought viciously.

Coy scowled.

"Listen," James said reasonably, "I figure you and me, we're the same."

"Same as copper and cowshit," Cord snapped.

James shrugged, too elaborately, so Cord saw the beginnings of doubt in his owly eyes. Cord liked watching those beginnings.

"I don't want to see you dead tomorrow," James said. "You and that handsome Mex lady. I'll bet she gives you a wild ride, and you wouldn't want that to end, would you? So you-all ride out and leave this train business to me. You get to live and rob more banks, and I don't have to worry about you getting lucky with some wild shot, hurting somebody—"

"Maybe just kill you," Cord said.

"That could happen, before you are dead yourself."

"You think anything, Coy?" Cord smiled at the fine-fingered man. "You know how to talk, Coy? I knew a man once got dropped on his head by his momma, and he never did talk. Just grunted all the time like a pig in a wallow, like all the time he was on the crapper. You simpleminded like that, Coy?"

Coy's hands slid back on the table until they were gripping the edge. Cord saw this was moving toward deadly now, and he did not care. He poured a fourth shot of bourbon whiskey.

"You think on this, Cord," James said.

"Have you spoken your piece?"

James frowned. This was not going his way.

"You got your whiskey. Get out." Cord put his own drink back in one quick motion.

When he lowered his head he was looking down a gun. Coy was out of his chair, and his pistol was leveled on Cord's gut.

There were a few drops of dark whiskey left in the heavy narrow bottom of the shotglass. Cord finished them, and hefted the glass in his hand.

"There is one more thing," James said.

Coy came around the table and stood not five feet from Cord. Cord tossed the shotglass easily in his right palm.

"You are standing between me and a lot of money, Mister Cord," James said. "You shoot faster than me, and you have been around and stayed alive. So you worry me, in a personal way."

Coy's gun did not move, but his eyes constantly darted from Cord's face to his hands and back.

"I don't want to think about you being underfoot tomorrow, nor me in your gunsight." Now the fear on James's face was obvious as a harelip.

There was the thing about back-shooters. They always figured everyone else was corrupt as they were.

"There is money in this for you," James said. "I'll wire it, anywhere you want, when this is done. I'll do it, because I won't want you hunting me."

Cord laughed. He tossed the shotglass on his palm again, and Coy watched it like a chicken watching the sun.

"You decide," James said. "Ride out, you and your partner, or you are dead, here and now."

Coy's shoulders twitched and went stiff.

Cord tossed the shotglass once more, easily, casually—and the glass arced toward Coy.

The man instinctively threw up his left hand, and the weapon in his right came up as well. In that same moment, Cord's gunhand swept back, his stiffened thumb catching the hammer of his Colt, so the revolver came up cocked.

Cord shot Coy in the throat. At five feet the heavy .45 slug blew a great chunk of muscle and artery out the back of his neck, and Coy whirled like a cripple-legged dancer and bounced off the table and onto the floor. The coffeepot tottered and went over; its hot, thick contents washed across the tabletop and over Coy's upturned face, washing away blood and leaving the flesh pinkened.

Con James stared white-faced. Cord pulled the hammer to full cock again. James lifted his hands above his head.

Cord almost shot him anyway.

Then, from down the street, came the eerie scream of the girl Aggie. Cord instantly imagined Chi's hands, petting the child, trying to make her well.

So he only gestured with the Colt. James never took his

eyes from it as he backed to the door and fumbled behind him for the latch, pushed it open against the wind.

Cord followed in time to see James leap into the saddle. Cord fired once over his head, just for the cruel pleasure of seeing James nearly topple from his horse in fright. Aggie screamed again in the night, and that took some of the satisfaction from the childish act.

The wind was nearly amok now, and powdery snow was drifted to the windowsills of the mercantile. Snow blew through the open doorway and sizzled against the stove. The gale was sucking the whiskey glow from Cord's belly.

That was easy to fix. Back behind the bar Cord poured another shot and felt better when it was in him. He stared at Coy's twisted body and suppressed a shudder. He was suffering from more than cold.

The showdown had been a stupid and risky play, drinking in the face of two guns, even in the hands of fools like these. It was time to begin reasoning some workable ways through the next fifteen or so hours.

Instead Cord said, "To hell with that," out loud, and had another drink of bourbon.

Chapter Twelve

CORD GOT COY'S BOOTS UNDER HIS ARMS AND skidded the body back through the mercantile like a travois. He dumped it about fifty yards from the building, far enough from the well so nothing would be contaminated come spring. By morning the corpse would be frozen hard as petrified wood. Cord peered into the night, trying to make out the prairie. He could not see anything, and when he turned he could not see the lights of the mercantile either, and he slipped into a moment of panic.

Everyone knew stories of whiteout blizzards, snow so thick and hard-driven the visibility at midday was no more than the length of two horses. Folks lost their bearings between house and privy, and were found dead only a few steps from their door-stoops.

But where Cord stood the wind was blocked somewhat by the building, and Cord made his way, head down, by following the trough he'd made dragging the corpse. Presently he blundered against the store's back door, his cheeks stinging with the cold.

Inside he poked up the fire. He found a sack of salt and dumped a few handfuls over the bloodstains on the floor planks. Then he began to drink in earnest.

Cord sipped at the whiskey steadily and with method. He placed a tumbler beside his shotglass, filled it from his canteen, and chased each sip of bourbon with a taste of water. After a time he began to get over his recklessness with Coy. It had worked out, and no profit teething on it. But still there was the anger: He was painted into a corner on this train business.

The whiskey room was shadowy and warm, the only light coming from the coal-oil lantern hanging from a hook in the ceiling, and the glow of the fire through the cracks around the stove door. Outside it was blowing cold death, but inside was cozy as a womb.

Cord recalled a woman he'd known, nearly seven years back, in Green River, Utah. Her name was Esther—Cord could not recall her back name—a jack Mormon, one of nine wives tending a farmer some twenty years older than she, so she knew only a taste of sleeping steady with a man. She was ready for the whole menu when Cord came along.

They spent near a month together before Cord and Chi moved on—there was no trouble with Chi over these women, that was part of their understanding—and it had been a fine and quiet time. The old Mormon never found out, and Esther told Cord she could live easier now that she had memories. Even years later, this Esther now and then came into his thoughts like a smiling guest.

Cord and the booze began toying with a thought: Maybe he would go back there when this was over, just from curiosity, or for the reassurance of finding one thread of continuity. Maybe he would even see her, and find things out. Maybe he would be met with her look of everlasting relief, her tanned face tight and pinched with her life's solitude but now opening, the lines flowing away as she realized it was him, come back.

Cord was enjoying this vision, turning it over and looking at it from all sides, when the door opened. He ignored it, happy in his dreamland and wishing no company. But soft steps moved across the room.

Mae Cornell untied her scarf and snapped it like a bullwhip.

Without looking up Cord said, crudely as he could make it, "What do you want?"

"We need to talk." The lower half of her face smiled, but her eyes were dark and hard as obsidian. She shrugged out of her heavy cloth coat and draped it over the bar. Underneath she wore a divided leather riding skirt, high-buttoned boots, and a heavy woolen man's shirt.

"Nope," Cord said. "Not at all."

"Warm," she said irrelevantly. She undid the top button of her shirt and the one below, so Cord could see the bony points of her collarbone.

Mae went around the bar and got herself a glass and filled it with colorless liquor. Cord smelled the juniper-berry odor of gin. Mae was facing him directly across the plank bar, leaning over her drink, her face a foot from Cord's. Another odor mixed in, the pepperminty smell of the scent she was wearing. It didn't go well with the bourbon either.

"Maybe you're right," Mae Cornell said. Her tone was low, aimed toward suggestive but too hard-edged to more than graze the target. "Some men don't have to talk. They make a woman understand in other ways. I like that kind."

The ends of her pinned-up hair were frizzy with melted snow. "Some men use their hands gentle as if they were petting a cat. Others get rough. They know what they are about and they use their hands, hard and mean and not caring what a woman wants." Her voice was thick with sex. "I like it rough as you can make it, Cord. I'd like to wear your mark. I'd like to look over my shoulder and see the red welts from your belt across my ass."

She put her hand over Cord's.

"Lady," Cord said icily, "I don't give a goddamn what you would like." Her hand was cold as a toad. "Make your point if you have one, then leave me to my drinking."

"That's not what you want. I can feel what you want to do to me."

She arched one of her fingers, then very quickly and hard as she could she drew the nail across the back of Cord's hand. Its sharpness cut skin and immediately there was a line of blood, an inch long and thin as thread.

Cord slapped her across the face, hard enough to snap her head around to one side, and instantly he felt acute surprise. How had she brought him so quickly to lost anger?

Mae turned her face slowly back to him. Her smile was thin as the blood-line on Cord's hand. His fingers were lividly outlined on her cheek, but she refrained from touching at the spot. Her hand was rock-steady when she refilled her glass. She picked up Cord's bottle and poured for him too, cool as the madam of a San Francisco whorehouse. She sipped gin, her eyes always on his.

"You haven't told him yet," she said. "Maybe you don't mean to."

"Is that what you want?"

"I told you what I want—from you." She smiled her frigid smile, but did not try to touch him again.

"I knew Kinsolving would never be able to pull it off," she said reasonably, "not even with you and your woman siding him. And yet there it was, that wonderful train, full of cash money and ripe as the Tree of Life. We've known about it for a while—Kinsolving tells me everything—and I had to do something, because I knew men who could pull it off."

"So you sold him out. Going to watch while they kill him?"

"Con won't hurt him. We worked it out. They'll tie him

up out of the way, and it will look like he tried to stop them. He'll be a hero, and the only one hurt will be J. C. Arbuckle. You got any sympathy for him?"

She tried to raise her glass, but Cord grabbed her wrist, hard enough to hurt her. No pain showed in her eyes. "You really believe that?" he snapped. "You know he is going to die."

Doubt flickered and passed as quickly in her expression.

"You will have killed him," Cord persisted, "same as if you pulled the trigger yourself."

Mae jerked her wrist free, slopping gin over Cord's hand. "Maybe I will." Her voice was hard as a man's, and thick with hatred. "Or maybe I will pull the trigger on you and that high-and-mighty woman of yours. No matter what happens to the old man, you two are going to die." She tossed her head angrily, and one wet strand of dark hair came loose from her pins. "You talk so noble about who lives and about selling out, but you are thieves like us, and no better in the eyes of anyone."

But then, dizzily as before, her tone changed again. "You can save yourself though. You can throw in with us." She tried her seductive smile once more. "You have been thinking on it. You have an idea how the wind blows, and you are coming to see it's the only way."

"Jesus," Cord breathed wearily. Of course she would see it that way: By her lights, Cord would not have withheld the fact of her betrayal from Kinsolving unless he saw a profit for himself.

"I talked it out with Con," she pressed. "You are in for a full share. The woman too, if that's how you want it."

"One thing to remember about a double-cross," Cord said. "It points eight ways at once."

Mae laughed gaily. "You can have me too. I'll be part of

your share. I'll do that woman of yours, and you can watch."

Cord grabbed her wrist again and walked her down the bar, picking up her coat and tossing it over her shoulders. She did not resist as he shoved her toward the door, but when he opened it she spun around to face him.

The look she gave him was full of triumph, as if she had cut through to a place where his vulnerability was revealed. "Everyone wants something," she breathed. "What do you want, Mister Cord?"

"You—out of my sight."

Her laughter was a joyous trill, as if he had paid her the prettiest of compliments. Its sound raked and teased at Cord as she faded into the awful night.

Chapter Thirteen

CORD HAD ANOTHER DRINK, BUT HIS RAGE would not flow back into the bottle. The liquor did not even warm him that he noticed. He wondered if there would come a time when his body would become inured to the bourbon's effect, when instead of into well-being and clarity the whiskey would take him only into the darker moments of his past, and into musings about the terrors of growing old as a gunslinger.

No longer would there be the long spells of sobriety

between the hard drinking bouts; he would drink more often until he was drinking all the time—like Kinsolving.

Men like that hung around saloons all over the West. They had wild, tangled, salt-and-pepper hair alive with lice and vermin, wispy long beards, and sunken eyes aglow with madness. Cord would join them, and wear a hat with the brim half-torn from the crown and baggy pissed-in pants which had been someone else's, and he would smell of bummed beer and his own excrement. He would sleep in rag bins and endure any degradation for the price of a drink, and each time he sucked on a begged cigarette he would cough up bloody sputum.

It was a maudlin drunk-man vision, and Cord blinked it away. He never knew which trapdoor in his mind might open when he was drinking, but under one of them was self-pity. He tried to smile at his own bathos, but his lips were cracked and dry and it wasn't funny. He gave up on smiling.

This was a night he needed the dreamless snorting slumber the whiskey brought; without it he would not drift off at all. He would take the next morning with a hangover over a night of wakefulness with his mind running faster and faster.

Going around to the outside stairway to the second floor, Cord hung close to the wall. His head down, he did not see the drift until he was into it, floundering near to his waist in dry snow light as baby breath. Cord went to one knee, gasping in surprise as he took some of the fine powder up his nostrils. He thrashed back to his feet and stomped up the stairs.

Four doors opened off the short corridor; the near one to his right was half-open. The light seeping out revealed that he was covered with snow. But the bourbon bottle was intact, and Cord was foolishly proud of that.

He was brushing snow off with his Stetson when Chi

called to him. Cord pushed tentatively into her room. Chi was on her bed, curled against the wall with her serape gathered around, her sombrero on a chair. The lamp was turned low and the fire had burned down to embers, so only when Chi shifted herself did Cord make out the girl Aggie asleep in her arms.

"Drunk?" Chi asked.

"Mostly."

She nodded, as if it were expected and okay. "Put out the lamp, *por favor*. The *muchacha* would not sleep in the darkness." The girl snuffled in her arms.

Cord soft-stepped across the room, cupped his hand behind the lamp's chimney, and blew out the wick. He did not want to leave the room. He was able to distinguish Chi's features in the glow of the coals.

"She has not spoken," Chi said.

"About . . ." Cord remembered Chi's fierce anger and did not know what words to use. Whenever they approached intimate talk his ease left him marooned. Ten years together, and he could never tell her what he thought.

"Not about anything," Chi said. "Since it happened, she is struck dumb." Chi paused, carefully framing her words. "Before she was full of wonder and craziness, but she could let some of it out with her strange talk. Now she has only fear, trapped inside her. Think of the horror, *querido*."

Cord started. She had never used the lover's term before; he would remember. Chi was different since this crazed girl. Before, she never had time for women her own age, let alone children. The child had awakened dormant feelings of maternity and womanhood. Cord was desperately uneasy with the idea.

He wanted to say something supportive, indicate his understanding. Instead he said, "Should I put on more wood?"

Chi shook her head.

Cord closed his eyes. *"Buenas noches."*

Chi said his name, soft as a caress.

"What?"

"Buenas noches," she whispered.

Cord's room was no warmer than outdoors and dark as a mine shaft. He groped to the table and found the lamp. Digging a lucifer from his vest pocket, he lighted it, then turned up the wick so the light reached out for the corners.

Mae Cornell was in his bed.

Cord felt paralyzed. As he stared she eased the blanket down. She did it slowly, showing him her small breasts with nipples hard from the cold, and then her stomach, ribbed like a washboard, and finally her sex, which was nearly hairless. All the while her eyes did not leave him, staring a challenge.

"This is what you wanted, Mister Cord. This was it from the moment you saw me." She licked at her lips and touched at her labia.

Her voice released him. Cord crossed the room in three steps, and as he came she put her arms up to him like some succubus.

Cord jerked her out of his bed. She went to her knees, but he yanked her upright. When she made her legs go limp, he dragged her. She tried to claw at him before Cord threw her out into the cold hallway.

She slammed against the far wall, arms outspread, her face and chest freckled with arousal, her breathing ragged.

"You move from there," Cord said, "I'll kill you." He was horrified, because it was true. Mae's taunting smile faded.

Cord gathered her clothes, hating the pepperminty smell, and flung them in her face. They fluttered to the floor. She watched him watch her nakedness.

Cord slammed the door and fell back against it, and waited until he heard her pad away down the hall. As he built a fire, he realized Chi had known; her hearing and instincts were phenomenal. What had Chi started to tell him?

Cord undressed and found his bed smelled of Mae Cornell. He rolled a cigarette, and the smoke cut some of her spoor from the air. The bourbon bottle was only a third full by the time he crushed out his smoke, but when he blew out the lamp he still could not sleep. So he relit it and got up and found the crushed Hamilton watch in his vest pocket.

He opened it and read Chi's inscription once more, and this time he was able to drop out of the world once he got into the warm darkness of his bed.

Chapter Fourteen

CORD AWAKENED BEFORE DAWN, AND MOSTLY clearheaded, which was a fine surprise. He rarely slept more than five or six hours; when he slept longer—out of trail fatigue or illness—he awoke ill-tempered and disoriented, and damned near every time ended up making some wrong move, or quarreling with Chi over something of no consequence.

It had to do, he supposed, with his first sixteen years growing up on that East Texas spread, where there was never enough daylight for chores. Those days bed became a campground for his frustration with his life, and sleep was like shameful retreat.

Cord had escaped and left his mother and father and brother Jim to that life, but it wasn't altogether in his family blood. When he was a child, his mother told him stories of her brother, named Childress, who one day had run off to New Orleans and shipped to Panama. There he was poled up the Chagres River in a dugout canoe by Indians, along the same route where they were talking now about cutting through a canal. On the Pacific side Childress had shipped to San Francisco and the goldfields of the Sierra Nevadas.

Uncle Childress had come back to Texas one time, when Cord was five. He stayed about six weeks, and Cord retained a vague image of him: big, long curly hair like Buffalo Bill in the lithographs, full of talk as much as Cord's father was full of silence. But Cord remembered clear as noon what Uncle Childress said when he left: "I am damned if I can even stand to watch people farming anymore." He was off back to the Sacramento Valley to keep case for a faro game on an upriver boat.

When he traveled to California the first time, Cord asked about this Childress, but nobody knew the name. Cord decided his uncle was either rich in some hilltop city, or more likely dead of a card-shuffler quarrel. It made Cord aware of the strain of chance running in his own life, so he thanked that long-lost and vaguely remembered Uncle Childress for the way his childhood visit had ended up steering Cord's own life.

But such musings wouldn't help this day. Cord swung out of bed and padded across the little room in his union suit, stirred up the coals, and added two split-wood chunks to the fire. He poured cold water from his canteen into a pan and sloshed some over his face, then quickly dressed. The boots he'd bought in Juárez were beginning to soften to his feet.

Last he strapped on his gunbelt, the leather soft with wear, and tied the rawhide thong around his thigh above the knee. He slipped the long-barreled Peacemaker out, cracked the cylinder, and rotated it between thumb and forefinger, checking the cartridges and the action. He thumbed the hammer to full cock and kept his thumb on it while he pulled the trigger, easing the hammer back to rest.

This was daily ritual, as prayer might have been. Partly it was seeing to his most important tool, and partly it was reassurance. Both were important for survival in the life he had chosen.

Cord stood at the window and watched the light gradually turn from near darkness to opaque white. The storm had continued to crescendo during the night, and now the whiteout blizzard Cord feared was almost on them. He could barely make out the sheriff's office; the livery down to his right faded in and out with the gusts, and the railroad depot was swallowed in the storm.

The boardwalk below was covered by a smooth drift that began in the street and swept up to the bottoms of the liquor room windows. Ridges of drift in the street shifted like ocean waves. A whirlwind of flurries formed from nowhere and went racing off down the street.

If the expected gunplay came off, it would be like fighting blindfolded in the dark. It would be a good time to keep a cool head.

At the foot of the outside stairway Cord had to kick a path through the drift to get into the merc. He refired the stove and had coffee boiling when Chi came in with Aggie. Chi spoke quietly to the girl, who earnestly shook her head yes and went into the back room.

"She's looking some better," Cord said.

"But she will not forget," Chi said. "Still hasn't spoken

either." She sat his coffee in front of him. "*Cómo está usted?*"

But she knew how he was; she still surprised Cord by how well she read him. She had heard the goings-on in his room the night before, what had happened and how angry he had been. The question was politeness.

"I'm okay," Cord said.

Chi reached across the table and traced one warm finger along the back of his hand, following the path of the scratch there. Her touch gave Cord a jolt, and he turned his hand and took hers and held it a moment, surprised at the bold intimacy.

"When this is over . . ." His voice was thick.

"We'll talk then." Still she did not draw her hand away, so after a moment Cord let go himself.

He wondered what would happen if he stood and dug his fingers into her hair and made a try at kissing her. Her eyes were glowing, like she might actually be hoping for such. They might kiss and lead each other out through the drifts and up to her bed, and tear away their clothes. . . .

And then what? They were comrades, ten years of covering each other. All that would be turned into some new and fragile relationship that would twist in the wind, like love always did. As partners they defended and forgave each other; neither might have the restraint to live with love.

Yet now Cord wanted it: honest, clean passion. It was a shocking thing to acknowledge. How long had he been denying these true feelings, pretending they did not exist?

Cord was relieved when Aggie came back from the other room, releasing from such introspection. The girl carried a jumble of cans for Chi's inspection: two tins of side pork, another of condensed milk. On her second trip she brought a bowl half-filled with grayish flour, a skillet, and forks and spoons. Chi pulled her knife to open the milk, but Aggie shook her head hard enough to whip her stringy hair from side to side. Chi gave her the knife and the girl went to work on the can herself.

Aggie knew what she was about, at least on this familiar ground of cooking. She fried up the salt pork, plopped dollops of batter into the grease for flapjacks, and set the plates before them. She watched and nibbled at her lip when Cord took his first bite, so he smiled and said, "Mmm, that's good," feeling clumsy with the compliment. But the girl was obviously pleased, and the food *was* good. Cord found he was immensely hungry.

Chi pushed her own plate toward the girl and said, "Eat, *niña.*" Aggie shook her head and returned to her cooking. Chi shrugged and dug in. "It takes her mind from the *diablos.*"

Tom Bowen came in as Aggie was refilling Cord's plate.

"*Buen día,*" Chi said.

"I want to talk."

"First eat," Chi said.

Bowen frowned, but took off his coat and drew up a chair. Aggie watched him. "It's all right, *muchacha,*" Chi said. "He is just one more for breakfast."

The girl went back to her cooking and forgot them. Cord ate more side pork and another big flapjack, then he and Chi drank coffee and smoked while Bowen and the girl ate. Aggie rushed through her food, jumping up to clear the table soon as she was done.

"He's not a bad man," Bowen said.

"All right," Cord said.

"You listen to me," Bowen said sharply. "When I came out here I'd been gone from Kentucky for three years and on the run all that time. A man had been robbed and shot, and it looked like it was my doing."

"Was it?"

"That's no question to ask. But no. Not that it made any difference, because everybody stood against me, even my own people. I lit out. The war was ended, and no work for anybody, so I became what they called me. I gave up notions of right and wrong in favor of living."

"Other men did the same," Cord said, "after the war."

"I wasn't a man." Bowen spoke too fast, as if, having to tell this, he wished to get it said quickly as possible. "I took up stealing and was no good at it. I was a boy, and they treated me like one when they caught me."

Aggie stood by the door to the back room, enrapt by Bowen's quick monotone. He frowned, as if he already had plenty enough audience for his taste. "They do not deal in legal finery like trials when handling teenage runaways. They beat me so bad I pissed blood, or saw two of things for weeks. They put me in jail, and sometimes that was the best I had lived for a while. A few times they chained me and made me work like a nigger slave. Knowing where I grew up, you can see where that would be worse than the beatings."

Cord understood: The deputy was not so much angry as unsure of himself, and he would always be that way until he knew how other men viewed up. His only way to manhood had been through force, and now he was not sure he had done right.

"When I left Kentucky," Bowen said, "I had nothing but my self-respect. That was gone by the time I came here. Kinsolving was an old man, by himself, and he took me in. I was standing on a cliff edge ready to dive off, and he turned my mind. That's it."

Aggie nodded thoughtfully, as if there were a special message in the story only her addled mind could divine.

"Actually," Bowen said, "I'm lying. He caught me trying to steal a horse. He knocked me over the head with his gunbarrel and I woke up in his jail. He told me he could see I was stealing for amateur reasons, like hunger and despair, and asked if I was ready to behave myself. I said I was, and he opened the cell door. First off I tried to punch him, so he knocked me out again.

"Next day," Bowen went on, "Kinsolving said, 'You didn't let me finish, boy. This time you hear me out, Tom Bowen. I got to pay for feeding prisoners out of my pay,' he said, 'so I ain't about to let you loaf around here. But you are also a young desperado, and I can't let you loose to terrorize the populace. So you are going to work for your keep, and if you try to run I will kick you around. Bye and bye you are going to do as you are told, or your head is going to crack open like a melon. You decide which.' "

Bowen rubbed the point of his chin with the back of his thumb. "I decided to stay around long enough to kill him. Turned out by the time I got the chance, I'd given up the idea. Meanwhile he knocked me ringy a few more times, but he never stopped treating me like a man."

"So after a while," Chi said, "you started seeing yourself that way. Is that it, *muchacho?*"

"Yeah," Bowen said. "It's one of the reasons I'm getting tired of that *muchacho* business."

"You're right," Chi said gravely. "I'll cut it out."

"Anyway, you ought to see where I stand. He was a good man, before that woman got under his skin with her ideas, and the drinking got so endless."

"Some woman," Cord said, remembering the sight of Mae Cornell in his bed.

"Don't be so sure she's all that pushed him into this. Maybe she was just first to speak it out loud."

There was a kind of inevitability to this, Cord saw. The debt he'd incurred twelve years back, Kinsolving's failures in the meantime, the dehorned boy Bowen had been when he stumbled into this place, and Mae Cornell drifting in and always open to chances for mischief. Too many people feeling bad about themselves and the world, and seeking a way to climb out of holes they'd dug themselves.

"He was the only one," Bowen said, "who laid eyes on me and did not write me off as a man. Don't be too quick to write him off, either."

Bowen might have had more to say, but something he saw over Cord's shoulder stopped him. A moment later Mae Cornell came in, John P. Kinsolving's bulk towering behind her. The old man looked better than he had any time since Cord had ridden in. There was character in his face and the flesh was not so puffy. He held himself loose and alert, ready in mind and body for whatever the day might drag in.

He grinned, confident and natural, then he clasped his hands together and dry-scrubbed them. He looked as pleased as if he were throwing a party and everyone had favored him by coming.

"So here we are," Kinsolving said grandly. "All washed and dressed, and ready to eat snakes."

Chapter Fifteen

KINSOLVING SHRUGGED OUT OF HIS HEAVY coat and sat down with Cord and Chi and took coffee, and at first only made small talk. But nobody else had much to say, and after a while neither did he. He was like a carnival barker who had gathered a crowd and then forgot his spiel. Silence thickened the tension, and Aggie grew increasingly distressed, leaning to Chi and plucking at her sleeve, making guttural meaningless sounds, her agitation the barometer of everyone's strain.

Bowen put on more coffee. The stove was already about hot as it got, and within a few minutes the thick dark brew boiled up and set the top ajar and oozed down the side of the pot to sizzle on the cast-iron stovetop. Bowen picked the pot up by its rag-wrapped handle and poured refills. Kinsolving put his hand palm-down over the top of his cup.

Chi came in from the back, hitching up her britches, and Kinsolving followed her with his eyes when she sat and bent to her steaming cup. Mae Cornell sat alone at the square table. She should have been locked up, Cord knew; her treachery was not half run out. But this had to be Kinsolving's show.

Mae had put her cool gaze on Chi right off when she and the sheriff came in. Chi returned a look of withering contempt, Chi's knowledge of what had happened in Cord's room showing plainly, scathingly. From then on, the other woman did not exist for Chi.

Kinsolving drained the lukewarm dregs of his coffee and went to the bar. He sat a bottle of the unlabeled whiskey and a scratched shotglass in front of himself on the plank trestle ostentatiously, as if challenging someone to object. Cord looked away. He knew it would be an awesomely piss-poor idea for Kinsolving to start drinking now, but he would not be the one to say it. If the old man had to fill his hollows with whiskey—even on this morning—it was his look-out.

But Kinsolving surprised Cord. He fooled with the bottle and the glass, turning them on the bar, tilting them to the light, and he occasionally glanced up to see if anybody had changed his mind in any way, but he did not drink.

It was somewhere near eleven, and the scene was static as a portrait. No one could pass the long waiting minutes before a shooting fight without getting some kind of fidgets, but Cord had some experience with this kind of thing and could handle it. He hoped Bowen was all right; he sensed that the deputy's constant frustration was strong enough to keep him sharp. Chi was no concern; in some ways she was cooler in gunplay than any man Cord had ever known. During the action her concentration was absolute, and she was emotionless as a trigger.

Kinsolving shifted his weight and a plank creaked under him. "What do you think, Cord?"

"We'll make your fight, John P. Beyond that, let it lie."

Kinsolving smiled. "I don't think so."

He rested one hand on the bottle's neck. "There are things owed a man," he said. "I am fifty-two years old and have not had my due. That is what this is about."

Bowen got up abruptly and carried his coffee to the end of the bar farthest from the rest of them. Cord suspected he'd heard this talk before and hated to see it start.

"A man is owed freedom and room to run," Kinsolving said. "But he needs the wherewithal too." He shot a look down the bar. "Isn't that your thought, Tom?"

Bowen did not look up.

"Wasn't it, Tom? When you come crawling into my town?" Kinsolving smiled and looked away reluctantly. "And isn't that what turned you to the gun, Cord, and you as well, Miss Chi? Nobody gives a handsome way of life over to you free and gratis. You got to be tough and savvy and grab what you want. They will try to stop you, but you have got to want it bad, and take it."

"No," Chi said. She stood. "You are a sad old man."

Cord had no idea what she was up to.

"Go for it." Chi's eyes were black with anger.

Kinsolving did not move.

Chi was poised to kill. "Go for it!"

Kinsolving lifted both hands in front of his face.

"That's right," Chi said. "Back down and have your drink. You're not taking anything from anybody. People are giving you their time as a gift, and you are spouting this horseshit. Go for your gun, so I can blow your fat carcass all over the bar."

Kinsolving lowered his hands to the planks, moving slowly. "What do you know?" He tilted the bottle and studied it. "I want a drink bad as I ever did. And that is bad as can be."

Cord regarded Chi, near quivering with anger. One moment she was acting like mother to the world, and the next she was mad as a coyote. But he had no doubt she would have killed if Kinsolving had made the slightest move for his gun. Nobody was due any slack in this kind of time, except what they earned with their speed of hand and quickness of mind. Now that point was underlined.

Kinsolving jerked the cork from the whiskey bottle and put it under his nose. He breathed deeply, shutting his eyes with the pleasure of it, like a Frenchman sniffing fine wine.

Then he began to pour. He did not stop when the shotglass was full. Whiskey slopped out over the bar and ran through the cracks onto the flooring, soaking into the old dry wood. Kinsolving did not stop until the bottle was empty. He recorked it and set it on the back shelf, and then he swept the puddle of whiskey away with his sleeve. The shotglass hit the floor with a dull clunk, pivoting on its bottom and rolling to a stop against the wall.

"Sure enough," Kinsolving said to Chi.

Slowly she let her right arm relax. Then she nodded and sat down again.

Mae Cornell eased behind Bowen and went to stand

beside Kinsolving. She laid a hand on his left arm in what
struck Cord as a crude parody of concern. Kinsolving
turned a tender look on her. "Even Mae here has got her
wants. You've learned like the rest of us, haven't you,
honey? Grab for the comforts."

Mae took her hand away. The smile had never left
Kinsolving's face.

"When I met you, Cord," he said, "I had already been
eight years down the trail. Eight years of banditry, and I
could not afford a plug of chaw. Sitting pretty!"

Kinsolving rubbed at his crooked left elbow. "One thing
a man has got to have, or at best you are broke and at worst
you are dead. You got it, Cord."

"What's that?"

"Outlaw luck. It shines on you like high sun in July,
while all my days I been in some snowbound Kansas."

Cord knew this wasn't true. You made your own luck,
and when you could not you made do. Grit had a hell of a
lot more to do with surviving, grit and the ability to stand
some bad times on the way. Grit was what Cord had and
Kinsolving did not, and maybe that was why they had split
trails twelve years back.

Yet on this morning Kinsolving seemed to have redis-
covered in his past a last reserve of determination, and was
driven by it as hard as the drinking and that damned Cornell
woman.

"That day in Red Bluff," Kinsolving said, "when those
men appeared on the rooftops, raining lead down on you
and me, horses snorting and wide-eyed and powder smoke
filling the street, and a forty-four slug from a Winchester
carbine burning in your gut—you recall that day, Cord?"

"Sure do, John P."

"It was always that way for me in my road-agent career.
Pain and pandemonium and always running, and nothing to

show for it but this twisted arm"—he gestured helplessly—
"and memories sour as alkali."

The whiskey had been with Kinsolving too long; he was
going through the stages Cord had seen the day before. He
no longer had to drink for his humors to skither from one
pole to another.

"You knew it back then, didn't you, Cord? There in the
Sierras, coming out of your fever and less than halfway
alive, you could still smell failure on me. That's why you
wouldn't partner up—not with a man whose luck and nerve
had run out long ago."

"Could be your nerve isn't quite so washed up as you
think."

Beside Cord, Aggie moaned. Chi petted her scraggly
hair, and the moaning abated.

"Could be," Kinsolving said expansively. "But that
don't matter anymore, because we are partnered up after all.
Twelve years later, and here we are." As if he had drunk
another shot, his voice went cocky, provoking. "All
partnered up, and nothing you can do about it, Cord. So
how is that for a pretty turn?"

"Watch yourself, *viejo*," Chi warned. "There is plenty
can be done about it. You can talk yourself into real trouble
yet, for starters."

But the sheriff was already careening off on another tack.
"I gave it up not long after Red Bluff. Spent three years
working cows in the country around Carson City, and hated
it. I was too old for taking orders, and pretty soon I would
be too stove-up for horseback work. I pictured myself
driving the chuckwagon, cooking and playing maid to the
young bucks. They would treat me like an old fool, like I
have treated cooks, and they would be right.

"So I drew my pay and carried it cross-country with
nothing in mind until I got to Hays City, here in Kansas. It

took me maybe six hours to lose most of it, bucking the tiger in the Rio Rita Saloon. I'd come all that way to find some Texican hands to ride with, and threw away my stake before I'd slept a night in town."

Kinsolving flexed the fingers of his right hand, then molded them around an imaginary gun butt. "But I also run into a piece of luck. That summer, Hays was the stomping ground for a Tennessean named Rennicky. This Rennicky figured himself a tough hombre and liked to provoke gunplay, but only with men who knew nothing about shooting. Which did not generally include Texicans. But he made an exception for me, seeing as how I was into my forties and going gray and long in the tooth. So Rennicky called me out."

Kinsolving smiled fondly. "I was always quick with a gun, and that never left me. And I had seen this Rennicky work. I could beat him easy, and there it was. Nerve didn't enter in.

"So Rennicky made his noises about showing an old man some tricks, and everyone trooped out into the street, dutiful as milk cows, to watch the blood flow. Rennicky went for his pistol and I shot him in the gut, easy as drilling a pie plate. He dropped his gun and clapped both hands over the hole, looking up to me like I'd tricked him. I shot him again in the middle of the chest, and he flopped backwards and quivered and was dead. Good riddance to trash."

Kinsolving was enjoying himself. "They made me town marshal. It was a likely prospect for me: I knew something of the law, for sure. And here is the funny thing: I took to the work. I was understanding, you might say, and kept most of the trouble moving right on through town.

"After Hays City," Kinsolving said, "there was other lawman work. Kansas was a growing state, with opportunities. I came to this Weed five years back, thinking it might be a good place to ease down into my quiet years. But now I can't stand the quiet."

"John P.," Cord said, "you ought to learn."

Kinsolving slapped a palm on the bar. "Goddamn it, no." Telling the story of his last moment of risk and triumph had only stiffened his resolve. "I was years an outlaw and nothing for it, and now I been years a law-dog and nothing for that either. Half a lifetime and all come down to this." His sweeping gesture took in the shabby barroom, and beyond: the treeless flatland of his impoverished domain, wind-curdled wintertime Kansas.

"I told you once, Cord: There are things owed a man. Today I will collect mine."

Aggie's teeth began to clack together loud as the lid atop the boiling coffeepot, her madness stirred by Kinsolving's own obsessions. Chi gently but firmly turned her head away from the sheriff's looming figure.

Kinsolving paid no attention. "For twenty years I been carrying life's paper." He was talking to Cord. "Today I am going to cash in. I am riding that train to grace and salvation."

Could be, Cord reckoned. In some ways he still liked the older man, but it was his experience that second chances could rarely be converted to advantage. Men like Kinsolving, who had been given their chance and lost, were too often contaminated by the habit of failure. He should have let it lie. There was too much riding on this last try, and that could be incapacitating; a man could freeze, like a boy facing his first woman.

And they would all be in trouble.

"Cord," Chi murmured. She was still mechanically stroking the quivering Aggie, but he knew her mind was down the same track as his. Yet he wanted to hear her say it.

"You are all paid up. No matter how you reckon the bill between you and the *viejo*, you do not owe him this."

Kinsolving and Mae were both watching narrowly, but Bowen would not look up.

"Go on," Cord said.

"You can stop this," Chi insisted. Aggie pulled her face up from Chi's breast; even she wanted to see this.

Maybe Chi was right. Back in Juárez it had seemed straightforward, an unequivocal matter of honor and debt. But maybe those old rules were too simple now for real life.

There were changes everywhere—too many people, churches, schools, railroads—more law of the kind written in courts, and less adherence to the man-on-man rules by which Cord and a few others had learned to live. In Cord's world formal law was mostly a rumor, and disputes were settled by simple contests conducted along clear rules.

But that world was fading quickly. Even now, stick a gun into a bank teller's face and word was out by telegraph before you crossed the county line. Every deputy in the West had your description, and manhunt gangs were blocking every route of escape. Before long, Cord's way of outlaw life would be impossible, except in snowstorm backland like this little Kansas town, where they might still imagine they were in the old days.

But Cord would not voice that as an excuse. Out loud it would sound crazy as it surely was.

He and Kinsolving were not the same: That was the thing to remember. Kinsolving's days were numbered, and there was no real reason to follow Kinsolving to defeat. The old man would die in the next few hours, unless he was touched by golden luck. Too many people needed him out of the road.

"Those *bandidos* camped out on the prairie," Cord said

carefully. "Con James and his bunch—how do you figure they came to be there?"

"Suppose you tell me."

"Why not ask the lady?"

Mae Cornell stepped away from Kinsolving, but the old man still held his grin. "I don't have to. I knew she was in with James, that she called them boys in on my train. There are names you can tag me with, but stupid ain't one of them."

For the first time Cord had the satisfaction of seeing the Cornell woman nonplussed.

"I'm an old man," Kinsolving said, "and not the stud I used to be, except I never was in the first place. So where would I get a woman like this one, except with some promise of money?"

Kinsolving looked to Mae with genuine fondness. "We had us some times, you and me. After we take care of your rough friends and tap that train, we'll have some more. Think about all that money, sugar. If I came away with it, that would turn your head a while longer, wouldn't it?"

Aggie began to sob. No one looked away from Kinsolving.

"Maybe I could have stopped her," he said. "Maybe I didn't bother. Having James here forces my hand, which is maybe what I wanted: the fight joined, and no way out. Hell, Cord, maybe I'm clear crazy. That's what you been figuring, isn't it?"

Kinsolving did not wait for an answer. "Crazy or not don't matter. You can fight—you and your woman and Tom Bowen here—or you can run. But you won't. You came here because I called, every damned one of you, because running is not in you."

He will have his fine moment, Cord thought. *Right now*

*he is more man than he ever was, and he has you right.
There will be no running this day.*

"Now then, Mister Cord, do you have a plan?"

Off across the prairie a train whistle cut the wind's howl. Chi was holding the weeping girl, but the tenderness in her look was for him.

"Yeah," Cord said. "I plan to live through this day."

"We will, *querido,*" Chi said.

Chapter Sixteen

THE WIND STAGGERED CORD AS HE WENT through the door, and he needed both hands and all his strength to pull it shut behind him. The storm had become the whiteout he had feared: Except for the bulk of the mercantile a few feet away, Cord was alone in a world of wind and nothing else. Snow everywhere, in his eyes and nose and mouth and part of every breath. Though it had to be near noon, the day was like dawn, and Cord was adrift in a strange place.

Yet he did not feel the dizzying alarm of the night before, out back of the merc. Cord was centered in his instincts now, and no longer concerned with any of the questions he had wrestled the last day or so. He thought only of warfare, his mind cold as the wind. Within him was great stillness.

Cord carried his Winchester Model 1873 lever-action rifle, with sixteen .44–40 cartridges in the tubular magazine and a seventeenth levered into the breech. One pocket of his heavy coat was weighted with reloads for the rifle, and the other held .45s for the Colt Peacemaker on his right hip. Seeing the target was the major problem. But on this day that would be everyone's problem. In the bosom of this incredible storm it was impossible not to feel some disorientation, but Cord had memorized the layout of the little town: the set of the buildings, the ways in and out, the places a man could find shelter or hide out. This was an old survival habit.

Still, Cord walked into the storm's confusion tentatively. Had he stopped in the middle of the street he would not have been able to see anything but whiteness. But then the sheriff's office loomed in front of him, and he was all right again. He went along the side facing the railroad depot, and around back found a rain barrel under a gutter pipe. Cord upended the barrel and brushed it clean of snow with a gloved hand. When he stood atop it, the building's flat roof was at his chin. Cord did not like resting the Winchester in the snow, but he needed both hands to pull himself atop the building. Soon as he was up he dusted the rifle clean and checked the action.

From off left Cord heard the wheel-clack of the train, the throaty chug of the steam engine. The sounds grew louder, then were overlayed by the wheezy sigh of air brakes. Somewhere over in the enveloping snow, the money train was stopped.

Cord got to one knee and the wind nearly knocked him off the roof. His breathing was labored and he felt a little muscle-tired; in this weather he would have to husband his strength and move with all possible economy. He rose cautiously to a crouch and duck-walked to the front lip of the flat roof. A plank creaked under him, whining like a wounded animal. The wind had swept the roof mostly clear.

Then, away from the train, Cord heard the nickering of a horse. He dropped to his stomach and pointed the Winchester into the storm's whiteness, the barrel cradled in the palm of his left hand, the curve of the walnut stock firm against his shoulder and his right cheek just brushing it, waiting for a target to materialize above the open sights.

The others would be in place. Bowen was in Chi's room above the merc, and Kinsolving had the window in the whiskey room below. Chi had put Aggie in the back room, with orders to duck behind the counter and stay put until Chi came to fetch her, no matter what else happened. That was a concern; the disturbed girl was apt to do sudden and dangerous things, and Cord did not want Chi's mind divided. This was a war; any lack of concentration cut the odds of living through.

Mae Cornell was in there as well, which was without question a danger of fair proportion. Chi had suggested, to Kinsolving's face, that they tie the woman and stuff maybe a half-yard of boltcloth in her mouth. Kinsolving gave the idea a few seconds of amused consideration before rejecting it. If he came out on top, he told Mae, she would still get her share and no strings attached, which was likely a better deal than Con James would give her. All Kinsolving asked was her word she would stay clear of the fight. Then, he pointed out wryly, no matter who won she came out ahead.

Mae gave her word, and Chi snorted, "The word of a *puta*, given to a *cornudo*." Mae tried to snap an answer, but Cord cut her off. "You keep this in mind, lady: The way things stand, considering how much I like staying alive, and the trash we are going against, your last best bet may be old John P. here, our man. And one more thing: You even think about any sort of back-shooting, and my partner is going to kill you. Right off, no questions. Bet money on it."

But now, lying flat on the roof of the sheriff's office and peering into the depths of the bottomless whiteout, Cord did not forget she was a potential extra gun against them.

The horsemen entering town were close enough now so Cord could hear their mounts' hooves crunching into the crusted crests of drifts in the street, and the murmur of someone swearing. The wind distorted all sound and even the direction from which it came, but Cord figured the riders at maybe fifty yards.

They would be strung taut as piano wire. Cord had ridden into strange towns with big-money thievery on his mind, and the tension was always worse than the actual doing—long as you survived. The blizzard would only make it worse: There was no comfort in knowing guns awaited you, and you unable to see ten feet ahead.

The wind slackened a touch and Cord got a glimpse of them. Con James headed the double file, his hat low against the storm but not so low Cord could not see his spectacles. Digger Dean, the black man who had needled Reuben C. Greyson into trying at Chi, was riding at his side. Among the seven others Cord made out Jasey Crook, the Fort Benton rustler, and Mac Cobb, the black Irishman.

All this Cord took in during the time necessary to draw a breath, let it half out, and squeeze the Winchester's trigger. Con James's gutty trunk sat above the bead of Cord's sight. It was not a long rifle shot; Cord could generally score fist-sized groupings at twice the distance.

But the blowing snow obscured his target at the last second, or sheared the slug a fraction off line, or Cord might have flinched from firing down on a man without warning—when it was added up, Cord had missed.

He swore and worked the lever, and a brass shell flew out past his cheek. Compensating for the wind and firing mostly blind, Cord ripped off another round. He heard a cry of pain and got a glimpse of a man-shape as it tumbled from the saddle. Across from Cord, Tom Bowen fired almost simultaneously, and another outlaw went down.

From behind the storm's white curtain Con James hollered, "Split up! They can't see any better 'n you."

"Time to move on," Cord muttered. He made his way knee-and-elbow to the rear edge of the roof, dropped the Winchester, and landed noiselessly beside it. Around on the street, riderless horses pounded past.

It was a cat-and-mouse game now. The play was to spy out James's gang before he was spotted himself. But Cord knew that this kind of storm could quit without warning, and that would change the rules real quickly.

As Cord came along the side of the sheriff's office, a voice hollered, "Over there! Holed up in that goddamned barroom."

The voice was maybe eight steps away, in the lee of the office's front.

Cord leaned the Winchester against the wall, drew his knife, and moved toward the sound. There was only the voice, and then in the space of one smooth cat-step he made out the man's back.

Cord cupped the man's chin in his left palm and jerked it back hard enough to pop the neck joint. The man opened his mouth and Cord felt hot breath and spittle on his hand, but before his quarry could cry out Cord drew the knife across the man's throat, starting under the left ear and coming all the way around under the extended chin. Blood spurted with enough pressure to wash Cord's arm with the warm, sticky fluid. Cord lowered the man to the ground; his blood steamed when it hit the snow. Cord drew his Colt.

Down toward the train, the silence was broken by a gunshot. Cord eased along the front of the sheriff's office, then darted across the open space separating it from the livery. As he made the barn the wind eased again, and the wall of white parted like a stage-curtain to reveal the bulk of the depot and the train beside it, a black engine tailed by a tender, Pullman car, and caboose. The window shades were drawn in the Pullman. The train might have been abandoned months back, its crew seized by some communal madness and run off into the prairie.

On the street near the depot a man lay facedown, snow already drifting against his body. Around his head it was the color of plum preserves. Shot by one of his pards, Cord guessed—but there was neither time nor reason to dwell on pointless mystery.

From the corner of his eye Cord caught movement and the gleam of gunmetal. Digger Dean was maybe ten paces away, his gun up, but the big black man rushed his shot. A slug whumped into the livery wall next to Cord's head, but by then he was steadying his own weapon. Cord had a fleeting impression of the man's face, shiny as patent leather, as if the Digger were sweating even in this tearing wind.

The black man was recocking his revolver when Cord shot him in the chest. Simultaneously a rifle cracked, and the dark face exploded out at Cord in a spray of bone and red and gray. The Digger's gun flew from his hand and he pitched forward so hard his big body bounced before settling into the snow's embrace.

The blizzard was easing. From the livery Cord could now make out the outline of the mercantile. Five of the James bunch were dead now, but it would only take a lucky shot from one of the remaining four to finish Cord—if his back showed in their sights. He wanted cover, pronto.

Behind him someone howled agony, though there was no shot. Cord spun into a crouch, cocking his Colt as he moved, sighting in on the form charging him—and came within a pound or two or trigger pull of shooting Aggie.

She passed so close the hem of her shapeless coat brushed Cord's leg: a wraithlike apparition looming out of the storm and fading back into its protection. Both her hands were buried somewhere under the ragged layers of her clothing. If she saw Cord she gave no sign.

Cord took a step after her—toward the livery—and caught a glimpse of another figure coming from the mercantile. This one he recognized instantly. It was Chi. Her gun was drawn, and she wore a look of such pain that Cord thought she was wounded. He felt vertiginous with panic. He could handle the idea of being stalked by men he could not see. But the fear of Chi injured sent sickness waving through his stomach.

But her voice was strong and steady. "*La niña*—she has a gun."

"Let's move," Cord snapped. The whiteout had come up again, but despite its shield Cord felt vulnerable, standing in the middle of the street. And he was still a little spooked by the image of Chi shot and bleeding. He moved toward the livery, Chi following.

"Cord!"

The shout came from toward the mercantile.

"Hold right there, Cord. I know you hear me."

It was Mae Cornell.

"Tell him," she said, speaking to someone else.

"She's got the drop." It was Kinsolving. "Her gun's in my back."

Should have roped her up, Cord thought. This was his fault. Deciding about Mae was where he should have taken control.

"You didn't have me figured fine as you thought, Mister

Cord." Mae Cornell laughed, shrill as the wind. "You were so sure I would double-cross Con for your side."

"Get it done with, Mae," James shouted from somewhere toward the far end of Weed, where he had ridden in not so many minutes before.

"Well, there you are, Cord," Mae snarled, ignoring James. "You are not so smart after all, and I am not such a turncoat. They call it honor among thieves. You ought to know."

This had mostly to do with him, Cord knew, and how he had thrown her out the night before, naked into the hallway and the cold. Kinsolving came into it too, because though he had slept with her, he'd known all along she was using him. She would despise him for that weakness—or was it strength? Who was used? Mae Cornell did not like men, and feared them because of it. Some men were the same with women, constantly anticipating betrayal.

"What do you want?" Cord called, and immediately moved five paces from there, Chi on his tail.

"Show yourself," Mae ordered. "Hands high and full of nothing."

"She's got us roped." Kinsolving's voice was dead, defeated. "We got no choice."

"The hell we don't," Chi muttered.

"Bowen?" Cord called, moving again.

"Shot up."

"Goddamned bitch," Chi swore under her breath.

"Listen to the lady, Cord," Con James called from down the street. "Do what she says and you will all live. Even the old man."

Cord knew that was the rankest horseshit. Even James would not expect him to believe it, but the man was out of better ideas and six of his crew were dead. And with the blizzard still howling around them, it was like fighting in a cocoon. None of them wanted to be the first to crawl out and show himself.

Cord took Chi's elbow and drew her back against the livery. "Go see to her," he whispered, his lips inches from her ear. She was no good if she was muddled up with worry for Aggie.

But Chi shook her head no, so Cord left it at that. He could not order her around. He had tried it once or twice in their early days, and learned right off there was plenty less trouble in letting her do as she pleased.

Maybe five slow-counted minutes passed, and no one moved, no one called out. The skin around Cord's eyes and nose, the only part of him not covered up, stung painfully and felt brittle enough to crack.

Then the wind began to ease, not in spurts of calm between heavy gusts as before, but gradually and steadily. The tail end of it was on them; Cord began to make out shapes: the sheriff's office and its barred windows, the two stories of the mercantile, the train to their back. There was still no sign of life from that quarter.

"Cord," Chi murmured. "Over there."

Mae Cornell was at the edge of the boardwalk. Kinsolving was on hands and knees in front of her, his crippled arm cocked like a dog's leg. His holster was empty; the gun Mae held down on him was his own.

Con James appeared from behind the far side of the building. He wiped at his streaked spectacles with the back of his sleeve, not bothering to remove them. He was flanked by Mac Cobb, Jasey Crook, and a man Cord recalled from the soddy because he had only one front tooth, and that one gold.

Everyone held guns, but Cord knew with hollow certainty he had lost the moment. He should have blasted them soon as they came into sight. But there was that goddamned woman, holding down on Kinsolving with his own gun. Soon as Cord fired, the old man would be dead. It would be the same as if he shot Kinsolving himself.

"Throw 'em down," Con James ordered, watching close through his owly eyes.

Disarmed they were dead. Cord knew that sure as sunup.

"I said throw 'em down." James grinned. "It is over for you."

Kinsolving had to know it as well. Could he anticipate the lead slug cutting his spine like fishline, the salty metallic taste of his own blood in his mouth before he drowned on it? The beaten old man raised his head and looked at Cord, and saw his death in Cord's eyes.

Kinsolving hollered *"No!"* as if he were denying the devil. He reared up on his knees like a great grizzly, twisted his heavy trunk and lunged at Mae's knees.

She danced back, but Kinsolving managed to hit her shin, and she yowled and stumbled. Her gun went off and snow puffed below the boardwalk. Kinsolving's knees were in the street and his trunk draped over the planks as he struggled against the slippery snow and his bad arm to regain his feet.

Cord shot the outlaw with the gold tooth. The man's knees buckled and he sat down in the snow almost comically and died that way, with his chin on his chest, like a dowager's escort at a charity symphony. Cord dove toward the sheriff's office, rolled, and came up with the Winchester he'd left leaning against the door.

Chi was on her stomach in the street, her Colt extended. She popped off a covering shot. James was lining on her when Cord brought up the rifle. Mac Cobb hurried a shot at him and turned tail toward the cover of the mercantile. Cord shot him in the back, and Cobb punched forward and slid along a few feet on his face before lying still.

James fired as Cord levered another cartridge into the

breech of the Winchester. A bullet tore a groove in the plank beside Cord, but then his rifle was up and steadied, and at the range of maybe thirty feet Cord could not miss. He shot Con James in the middle of his chest. James punched back and caromed off the corner of the mercantile. For a moment his spectacles hung crazily from one ear, before jarring off and sinking out of sight in the soft snow beside his head.

Jasey Crook screamed like a woman. He threw down his gun; his hands shot up and he stared whitely at Cord, backing away until he reached the corner of the building, then fleeing around it in hot panic.

Across from Cord, Mae Cornell screamed, "You cockless bastard!"

She was backed up against the mercantile's window. Kinsolving was making his feet.

Mae Cornell used both thumbs to haul back the hammer of the sheriff's big .45, extended it stiff-armed in front of her. Kinsolving froze—then lumbered at her.

Mae fired.

Kinsolving whirled around on tangled legs and tripped off the boardwalk. He lay on his side in the snow, his eyes screwed up shut.

Mae Cornell walked stiffly forward, recocking the .45. She bent at the waist, so the gun's muzzle was no more than three feet from Kinsolving's head.

The sheriff opened his eyes as her finger whitened on the trigger.

Cord squeezed off a shot.

Mae Cornell's hands flew up as if in supplication, and at the top of their arc the heavy revolver flew free and crashed through the whiskey room's window. There was blood high up on the front of Mae's coat, at the base of her neck. She pivoted gracefully on one foot and managed one step of escape before she toppled forward. To Cord at that moment she looked fragile and light as an autumn leaf. She fell so her neck landed on the sill of the broken window, and a shard of glass the size and shape of a fence picket stabbed into her throat.

As Cord drew himself to his feet there was a commotion of horse hooves. Jasey Crooks was racing out of Weed in the direction from which they had all come.

Chi picked herself up from the middle of the street and dusted snow from the front of her serape.

There was one last gunshot, from inside the livery. Chi let out a wail unlike any sound Cord had ever heard from her, and raced toward the sound.

Bodies littered the street, and snow drifted over the corpses and the thick bloody stains around them. Kinsolving was sitting up with his back against the boardwalk. He held his right arm cradled in his left hand; blood oozed out between his fingers. He was pale, his face composed. Cord did not know if he had turned to take in the grotesquely impaled figure of Mae Cornell.

Cord felt queer. He had never shot a woman before. If there was ever one who needed killing, it was Mae Cornell—and anyway she had been a heartbeat away from murdering Kinsolving, in cold blood and for perverse reasons that had nothing to do with the man himself or even that goddamned money train. Cord had no alternative—but still, he had never shot a woman before.

Kinsolving closed his eyes serenely, as if everything would be better after a little sleep, and Cord turned away from him and went toward the livery. He started to pull his Colt but did not, unaccountably angry at the gesture. *They are all dead now*, he thought. *The time for guns is past.*

Chi was in the far stall, where Reuben Greyson had met his end. Aggie was cradled in her arms, and for a moment Cord thought the girl was sleeping, or passed out from fright, or collapsed senseless into a madwoman vision. But then he saw the revolver in the girl's limp fingers, and the blood. There was a lot, almost too much to have been contained in the girl's slender body. There were puddles of blood in the hay, splashes on the stable wall, a great smear of it across the front of Chi's serape. Blood shone like a blackish red skullcap on the back of Aggie's head. There the bullet had exited, after the girl put the gun barrel in her mouth like an obscenity and pulled the trigger.

Chi looked up to Cord and tried to say something. Tears ran streaks down her face, and all that came from her mouth was a hopeless choking sob. Cord could not stand seeing her like this.

He should have taken care. These things were his fault. He was older and knew better, and he should have taken care. He wanted to tell Chi: From here on all of it would be different. For the two of them, it would change and be all right.

Chi sobbed, and Cord felt more helpless than ever before in his life.

Chapter Seventeen

EIGHT MEN WERE LINED UP IN FRONT OF THE Pullman, dressed identically in narrow-brimmed felt derbies with a subdued gray ribbon around the crown; a gray woolen scarf tied around the neck and tucked inside a long-skirted gray topcoat; and vulcanized rubber galoshes with metal buckles. On the lapel of each greatcoat was a shield-shaped silver badge. Each man was vaguely youthful and had an unlined featureless face, and each stood with legs slightly apart and held a 12-gauge shotgun at port arms. They looked to Cord to be posing for a picture.

Around the locomotive the trainmen had emerged. They wore coveralls over heavy union suits, and looked over their shoulders with frightened expressions, hoping that eight armed guards were enough force to hold off whatever crazies were out there in the Kansas snow. The fireman and engineer were chucking cordwood into the tender from an elevated snow-covered bin, while the brakeman got his fire built in the pan under the water tower and fretted around the spout, waiting for the ice to melt enough to start the flow. The conductor watched the others work, and all of them were real careful not to look at the dead men scattered up and down the street. After this run was over, Cord pictured them jawing about this, shaking their heads and saying, "They don't pay me enough to get shot up by them desperadoes," all the time secretly pleased at the chance to stand tall in the regard of other men.

None of the Pinkertons moved or even met Cord's eye as he approached. They might have been figures in a wax museum, fascinating but not altogether perfect reproductions of living people. Cord put his fists on his hips and said, " 'Lo there, boys," expecting no answer and not disappointed.

Then the door at the other end of the Pullman slid open and a ninth man swung down. He was dressed like the others but carried no shotgun. He might have been twenty-five.

This man took his time looking all around, saving Cord

for last. "Sheriff Kinsolving?" He had a flat, unaccented voice; Cord imagined that back in New York this man went places where that sort of voice was considered cultured. There were women who would get fluttery-featured and wet at a voice like that. Cord was feeling raw-rubbed around the edges. Seeing Mae Cornell guillotined on that shard of glass frightened him in some unfamiliar way, and he did not like it one bit.

"I'm Kinsolving." The sheriff came up beside Cord. He was still holding his bloody right arm, and his face was pasty from incipient shock.

"You all right, John P.?" Cord said.

"Actually," Kinsolving said, "no. My goddamned arm is broken." He took away his hand and Cord saw the splinter of armbone cutting through the skin, where Mae Cornell's bullet had hit.

The Pinkerton man looked on with a faint expression of distaste, as if someone had just shown him a daguerreotype he considered less than proper.

The weather was breaking for certain. A flicker of blue sky showed above the western horizon, and the wind was down. If it cleared, the night would be impossibly cold.

Kinsolving stared at his broken arm. "Well, Cord," he said, "I reckon we are going to have to pass up this train after all."

"Looks that way, John P."

The Pinkerton man frowned. "My sympathies on your injury, Sheriff. My name is Richard Warren, Pinkerton National Detective Agency, New York City." He offered his hand.

Kinsolving gave it a disgusted look and spit. He did not hit it, but he came close.

Warren lowered it. "I see," he said.

"You don't see one goddamned thing," Kinsolving said.

Warren might not have heard. "On behalf of Mister Allan Pinkerton and Mister J. C. Arbuckle, thank you for your efforts on their behalf."

Kinsolving ran his hard gaze up and down the line of men. "These pups know how to use them popguns?"

Warren stiffened. "My orders are to protect this train, sir. Without fuel or water we were stopped, and that put us in a difficult position. My only choice was a defensive stand until this . . . siege was over."

"Nine men with scatterguns . . ."

"There are fifteen of us, sir."

"Yes," Kinsolving said, "and you could not spare three or four. People died out there, and not all of them deserved to. Because you had orders to follow."

"I determined that I required my entire force to protect my cargo." Warren's tone was patient, tolerant. "We had no idea what was going on, or who might be involved." He looked at Cord. "Nor what threat they might represent."

"Come on, John P.," Cord said. "Let's see to that arm."

Warren stood more erect. "I can assure you, Sheriff, that your bravery and sacrifice will be duly noted in my report."

"You little ass-wipe," Kinsolving snarled. He tried to swing on Warren with his left, but the Pinkerton pulled back his head and Kinsolving's fist sailed harmlessly under his chin. Kinsolving's legs went rubbery. His eyes turned up in his head and he staggered backward. Cord caught him under the arms and nearly went down himself under the bulk.

Warren turned his flawlessly neutral eyes on Cord. "It's good to know there won't be more trouble," he said in his controlled voice. "The cars are armor-plated, we have repeating rifles and grenades, and food and water for two weeks. We came into this country prepared." He turned, thought better of it, turned back. "Let the savages fight one another." His gaze traveled over the street and the bodies of the dead, and ended on Cord. He smiled politely and turned his back, and there was little doubt which savages he meant.

Chapter Eighteen

T HE LAST OF THE STORM MOVED EAST DURING the night, and the morning dawned clear and crystalline cold, the air still, the sky brilliantly blue, and the sun coming up like a lost son returning to family. A thick, brittle sheath of frost covered everything.

Cord was sweating. He had spent the better part of the last three hours with an axe, cutting Aggie's grave out of the frozen prairie sod behind the livery, not far from Coffee River. The work was hard and the trench was only four feet deep when Cord gave it up. He did not like to leave the job until it was done right, but the axe handle was raising blisters on his gunhand.

There was a lesson from the last two days: You could not always finish things in a purely proper way. You try your best to help an old man salvage his life, and a crazed girl takes her own. Maybe, Cord thought, he *was* at fault. Maybe he was changing.

The girl's body was wrapped in a blanket, and Cord left it that way when he lowered it into the grave. But before he clambered out, something made him bend and pull back the rough wool to look at her face. It was the face of someone he had never seen before. In his discomfort he had not seen beyond the superficialities of the girl's ragged clothing and limp clump of ratty hair. Her face had calmed into serenity; in death there was no madness.

Cord covered the body with frozen blocks of sod, as if building a crypt. When he finished it was hours past sunup. Cord took off his hat and stood a moment.

"Good Lord," he said, "keep the wolves away."

Chi had the horses grained and saddled and hitched in front of Kinsolving's office when Cord walked back into town. The bodies were gone off the street. That had been Cord's job too, as the only able-bodied man in Weed. He looped his riata around a leg and dragged each body off to a pile out back of the mercantile; Kinsolving would have to see to them beyond that. It would be hell if the dogs got into them, or if a thaw came in. But that was not Cord's problem.

The only body Cord had not dealt with was Mae Cornell's. But it was gone, moved some time after the fight while Cord sat alone in his room, taking long pulls on the best whiskey he could find. Maybe Chi had done it, for reasons Cord would not guess at. He did not care.

Chi said nothing when he came back from the burying. She had been nearly silent since Aggie's death. It would be some time before she forgot. Memories would stalk Cord too. He saw Mae slumped over the broken glass and felt sick, at having killed her, or at the pleasure he feared he might have taken in the act. He could have saved her by roping her up in the beginning.

Cord frowned at the tricks his mind was playing.

Kinsolving was bedded down alone in his cabin. Cord banged at the door, then pushed in.

One of the Pinkerton men had come off the train and set

the arm, doing a fine, professional job so far as Cord could judge. It figured they would be traveling with their own medical man. The old man was gray and weak, but he would be all right, Cord guessed. There was a stack of firewood and plenty of food, and he had nothing to do but take care of himself and ruminate.

"You stay off the whiskey," Cord said. "Pretty soon you are going to be a hero. That Pinkerton, the kid boss, he said he wired your story back East, and there is going to be some kind of reward. They'll be writing dime novels about you— *John P. Kinsolving: The Last Good Gunslinger.*"

Kinsolving grinned thinly. "Seems right."

Chi was waiting out front.

"Unless you got more good-byes to make," Cord said.

"Let's ride." But then she reconsidered. "The *muchacho*, the deputy."

Tom Bowen came out of the mercantile to meet them. The right side of his head was wrapped in gray gauze spotted with blood. Mae Cornell had clipped his temple with a bullet, and he'd been out cold for the better part of the previous afternoon. The unfocused look in his eyes told Cord he had suffered a concussion. It wouldn't do any permanent damage. The deputy's horse was saddled and picketed next to Cord's gelding, the saddlebags bulging with gear.

"You going to ride with that head?" Cord asked.

"That's right."

"Save you some hurt if you wait a day or so."

The front window of the liquor room was boarded up, but Bowen looked at it like it was still clear glass. "I been hurt before," he said. "Best thing for it now is to get clear of this Weed town."

"Ride with us," Chi offered.

Bowen shook his head no and winced. "From here on, I'll be taking another trail."

They were in the saddle when Kinsolving came out of his log cabin. Cord wondered about leaving the old man, but supposed he could see to himself by now. It looked like Kinsolving's gunhand days were over, but maybe he would find another lucky life. Maybe someone *would* write a novel about the old man. More likely he would die as Aggie had, because his life had run out of possibilities.

Cord worried more about himself and Chi. This time out they had both admitted things previously left unacknowledged. Chi had come back to feelings long put aside, and he had examined feelings long suppressed. Now they were out, and with them questions that would need some pondering— about the life he had invented for himself, and his relationship with the woman he had chosen to share it.

Kinsolving pushed out of his office, a half-empty whiskey bottle in his left hand. There was no drink in his eyes, only sadness and pain. Cord thought of Kinsolving as a man on an island, jumping and shouting and firing gunshots to attract attention but the ships always passing on by. Kinsolving opened his mouth and closed it again without speaking.

Then he took a short sip from the bottle, and another, and defiance replaced the hurt in his eyes.

"Well, son of a bitch," he called across the street. "I'll wait for those fellows to make me a hero, but I won't wait long." He turned and slammed the door shut behind him.

Cord stepped up on the gelding, and Chi followed him out onto the long snowfields of Kansas.

Afterword: An Historical Note

ABOUT THIRTY MILES EAST OF OUR OFFICE IN Missoula, Montana, upstream on the Clark Fork of the Columbia, is the Burlington Northern Railroad siding of Bearmouth. It is identifiable by a trackside sign visible from the interstate, though trains no longer stop there. But in the first decade of this century, when the BN was the Northern Pacific, Bearmouth was a watering stop and terminus for shipments from the mining camps at Garnet and Coloma, twenty miles north into the mountains.

On the evening of June 16, 1904, while an NP train was making the Bearmouth water stop, two men came out of the dark and threw down on engineer Thomas H. Wade and fireman L. S. Reed. The one who did the talking wore a black hood, a grain sack with armholes cut into it, and two leather bags tied to his belt. He ordered Wade to douse the engine's kerosene headlight. Then he reached under the grain sack, brought out a cigar, and ordered Wade to light up.

Wade, like every other NP trainman, was acutely mindful of a successful robbery about a year and a half earlier at the same spot—by a black-hooded bandit who had offered the engineer a cigar. That engineer, Dan O'Neal, had resisted and was shot dead.

Wade lit up and blew out vigorous plumes of smoke.

While his partner covered fireman Reed, the leader walked Wade down the track to the express car. The expressman refused to answer Wade's repeated knockings, so the robber produced a stick of dynamite and set it on the car's doorsill. He ordered Wade to light the fuse, at which point the cigar finally made sense to the engineer.

The explosion blew away the door and a good part of the wall. Warning Wade to keep puffing, the bandit waved the expressman out of the car and set another stick of dynamite against the large safe. Wade balked at lighting this one, because he thought the fuse was dangerously short.

"Don't worry," the robber told him. "I've done this before."

The second explosion blew the safe through the wall, and the bandits recovered several thousand dollars in currency and gold before disappearing into the night.

When official authorities gave up on the search, it was put under the charge of Joel S. Hindman, an operative of NP's internal detective force. Hindman circulated posters suggesting that the bandits might be spending lavishly, and that turned out to be the key. An informer in Spokane, Washington, tipped Hindman to George Hammond and John Christie. After investigating, Hindman arrested Hammond. In his boardinghouse room Hindman found seventeen unmounted diamonds, weapons and ammunition, and a large number of greenbacks, some scorched. Under Hindman's relentless interrogation, Hammond admitted his guilt and implicated Christie, who was arrested the same day in Hope, North Dakota, after Hindman wired local authorities.

Hammond's outlaw playfulness extended beyond the cigar trick. In his confession he told of camping one night after the Bearmouth heist, near the summit of Black Mountain. For some reason—nerves, maybe—he and Christie quarreled. Hammond suggested they cool down by counting the lights of Missoula, lying below. After the count passed one thousand, Hammond pulled his revolver and threatened to shoot Christie on the spot. Christie ripped open his shirt and challenged Hammond to make good. At this point, according to Hammond, both men burst into laughter. Thus do outlaws have fun.

Hammond was extradited to Missoula on an NP train which happened to include the private car of Harry Horn, NP general manager. Out of curiosity, Horn had Hammond brought in and the two took lunch together. Horn wrote later that Hammond promised to be a friend to the NP from that day on. As far as is known, Hammond kept his word. He spent the next fifteen years in the state prison in Deer Lodge and came out with no more outlaw dreams—or at least none that he enacted.

There is vague anecdotal evidence that trains were held up in the South as early as the 1850s, but the invention of peacetime train robbery is generally credited to the Reno brothers—John, Frank, William, and Simeon—four unlikable thugs from near Seymour, Indiana. On October 6, 1866, the Reno boys took about $10,000 from an Adams Express Company car on an Ohio and Mississippi Railroad train. It was a tough break for Adams, but a lucky one for Allan Pinkerton, whose Pinkerton National Detective Agency ("We Never Sleep" remains the company motto) was the closest thing to a nationwide law-enforcement body until the twentieth century. Pinkerton's company would build its reputation on the apprehension of bank and train robbers.

Soon after the Seymour job, the Reno brothers took more than $22,000 from the Daviess County (Missouri) Treasury. A few weeks later John Reno was nabbed by Allan Pinkerton and six other men on the platform of the Seymour train station, and smuggled back to Missouri to stand trial. "It was kidnapping," Pinkerton later wrote, "but the ends justified the means." In Missouri, John was sentenced to forty years at hard labor, which would turn out to be a good deal in comparison with his brothers' fate.

The remaining Renos' most successful train job took place on Friday, May 22, 1868, when they stole $96,000 in gold and government-bearer bonds from a Jefferson, Missouri, and Indianapolis train near Marshfield, Indiana, bettering by a factor of three the previous record for train-robbery proceeds. But before the year was out, Pinkertons had tracked down Frank, William, and Simeon and returned them to New Albany, Indiana, to await trial.

On the night of December 11, 1868, scarlet-masked members of the Southern Indiana Vigilance Committee broke into the jail and lynched the Renos, one at a time. John was doing hard time in the Missouri State Prison, and this made it harder. "The awful news came near to dethroning my reason," he wrote in his autobiography, "but I was kept hard at work which saved me."

Train robbery became a uniquely American enterprise; in no other country was it ever a significant law-enforcement problem. In Great Britain, for instance, the first nation to develop successful commercial railroads, train robbery was rare. Most British track ran through heavily populated areas, affording greater security, and Britain had a coordinated national network of police forces. British trains did have a serious problem with what we think of as urban crime: assault, rape, robbery at weapon-point, and murder, perpetrated against first-class passengers as early as the 1860s.

In this country, train robbery was particularly attractive in the West. Often cut off from civilization for stretches of several hundred miles, trains were vulnerable. There was little chance of interference by the law or public-spirited citizens. In some ways trains were easier to take than banks, and unlike banks were accessible at night. And to paraphrase Willie Sutton, trains were where the money was.

Express cars were usually coupled directly behind the coal tender. Express companies were independent of the railroads, although their employees—called "agents" or "messengers"—were considered "railroad men." The agent's job was to accept or unload consigned goods at stations, and maintain records and waybills. For about forty years beginning in the 1870s, after stagecoaches and Pony Express and before airlines and telegraphic bank transfers, railway express was the only way to ship currency, coinage, jewelry, and other negotiable valuables.

Today it is difficult to pinpoint the amount actually taken in many train jobs. Figures varied even at the time, depending on who was doing the reporting. Robbers tended to boost the amount during barroom boasting and reduce it during courtroom pleading. Reporters inflated the numbers to sell newspapers, while express companies understated losses to maintain customer confidence. Conflict between express companies and the press on this issue caused some companies to clam up altogether. Of the Wells, Fargo chief of detectives, one reporter wrote, "Anyone who can get information from Mr. Hume has got to have a stomach pump and chemicals."

Passengers were less often robbed, and the U.S. mail was almost never touched. Coach riders were too unpredictable, particularly in the years immediately after the Civil War, when many were young combat veterans possibly given to heroics. Also, many outlaws enjoyed public sympathy born of widespread outrage at railroad land-grabbing, and did not want to jeopardize their reputations as Robin Hood figures.

As for registered mail, it was a hit-or-miss proposition, and a Federal rap.

The classical robbery required six men. Two boarded the train—at a station, water stop, or when it slowed on a long grade. Or the robbers might wave a red lantern; they knew it was a firing offense for an engineer to ignore a signal, even if he believed it spurious. The two front-end men would throw down on the engineer and fireman. A second pair flanked the train and guarded against interference from the conductor or passengers, and held the horses. The third pair saw to the business of neutralizing the express agent and lifting his valuables.

There was the tricky part. The easiest way was to persuade the messenger to open the car door and the safe, and behave himself. Threatening to set the car afire, or kill members of the crew, sometimes worked—and when the door was opened, sending in a crew member first was a sensible way to gauge the messenger's propensity for gunplay. Riddling the express car with bullets usually softened up a recalcitrant messenger.

Then there was dynamite. Few train bandits were expert with explosives. They might use too little and not breach the car, or more commonly too much, variously blowing up themselves, the express agent, or the safe and its contents. On June 2, 1899, for example, in the holdup of the Union Pacific's Overland Flyer near Wilcox, Wyoming, Butch Cassidy's Wild Bunch placed ten pounds of dynamite on top of an express company safe. The explosion destroyed the strongbox and most of the car, and scattered currency along thirty yards of track. Some of the bills were sticky when the Bunch gathered them up; the blast had also turned a consignment of raspberries into jam.

The most vicious way to rob a train was to wreck it, then pick through the demolished express car at leisure. There were three popular ways to derail a train: by opening a switch halfway; by barricading the track; and by unbolting a section of rail, attaching a wire, and jerking the section out just before the engine reached it.

In September of 1891, a Santa Fe train carrying over $1 million in cash was derailed at the top of the grade near Osage, Kansas. The engine and every car left the track in a wreck so total the outlaws were unable to reach the express car. Five years later, bandits wrecked a Louisville and Nashville train on a bridge over the Cahaba River—only to discover they had the wrong train. This one was chartered and conveying 35 members of a fraternal order on an outing, and did not even include an express car. The disaster killed 27 passengers and three crewmen, and the wreckers looted the bodies.

Wrecks were easy to accomplish and difficult to prevent. According to the U.S. Census, there were 8,216 train accidents in 1875 alone. But one train-wrecking story is cheering, because it had a happy ending and did not happen anyway. Probably. If it did, it was on the NP line near Medicine Hat, Montana, in 1892.

According to the Medicine Hat telegrapher, he was overcome one stormy night by a gang of masked men, one of whom knew telegraphy. Using the depot's key, this man revised the schedules of two express-car trains—so they would crash head-on at the depot. But just as he finished, a bolt of lightning struck the telegraph pole outside, starting a brush fire and electrocuting the badman. The rest of the gang contemplated their fried companion, still smoldering in his chair, and lost all stomach for their work. As soon as they rode off, the telegrapher ran out with a red lantern, but both engineers had spotted the brush fire and already stopped.

Another whimsical story of a train robbery gone wrong,

this one documented, occurred in California's Sacramento Valley. It devolved from the partnership of Jack Brady and Sam Browning.

Superficially, Brady and Browning's career was neither noteworthy nor successful. It began on the night of October 11, 1894, when near Mikon they took about $50,000 in gold and silver coins from the Southern Pacific's Overland Express. The following March, Brady and Browning stopped the SP's No. 3 and No. 5 passenger trains, and were thwarted both times by large safes and not enough dynamite. When the same thing happened a third time on March 30, they determined to rob the passengers. After netting about $1,000 and fifteen watches in the day coach, they moved on to the Pullman.

One of the passengers in that car was John J. Bogard, sheriff of Tehama County. When the robbers came in, Bogard shot Browning above the heart. Brady killed Bogard and fled. But before dying, Browning identified his partner. Brady was arrested four months later, convicted, and sentenced to life in Folsom. He was paroled in 1913 and died a few years later near Galt, California.

The figure who made the Brady-Browning story noteworthy did not emerge until almost two years after Brady's imprisonment. He was a hobo named John P. Harmans and known as Karl the Tramp, who was sleeping beside the SP trains the night Brady and Browning made that first $50,000 heist.

When Brady and Browning detrained with the loot, the noise awakened Karl. He watched from hiding while the two buried the coins. When they left he dug the proceeds up, extracted $10,000, and reburied the rest in a different spot.

Karl went to San Francisco, rented a Nob Hill apartment, styled himself Carl Hermann, and had himself a time. The money bought clothing, liquor, friends, and women. About the time it was giving out, San Francisco police got wind of his high living and became curious about its source. Before he could be questioned, Karl left the Bay Area and went back to hoboing.

Karl never touched the remaining $40,000. When he was arrested in March, 1896, he cheerfully revealed where it was buried. For illegally converting funds to his use, Karl was convicted of grand larceny on April 30 before Sacramento County Superior Court Judge Hinkson. In light of Karl's cooperation and the recovery of four-fifths of the take, Hinkson heeded a plea for leniency and sentenced Karl to three years in Folsom.

Before Karl was removed from the courtroom, Judge Hinkson asked if he had anything to say.

"Yeah," said Karl the Tramp with a faraway smile. "I lived like a prince."

Karl served two years before he was paroled, then hit the rails and was never heard of again.

In 1869 the first transcontinental rail-line was completed at Promontory, Utah. By 1893, all the major present-day western long-haul lines were in place. The Union Pacific ran from Missouri to the Pacific Northwest, with branches south to Texas and New Mexico. Southern Pacific lines connected the major California cities and went from the West Coast to New Orleans. From Chicago, the Great Northern ran west to Seattle, and the Atchison, Topeka & Santa Fe south to Los Angeles.

With so many opportunities available, train robbery became the crime of choice for many premier outlaws, including the James, Dalton, and Younger gangs, as well as Sam Bass, Bill Doolin, and the Wild Bunch. Train robbery also attracted some less well known desperadoes.

One was Bill Miner, who robbed his first train in 1869 and his last in 1911, when he was sixty-four. Another, with the unlikely name of Marion Hedgepeth, habitually wore a blue suit, white shirt, and derby hat; he was the best-dressed of outlaws, and among the quickest draws and most vicious killers. Or consider Sacramento Valley train robber Chris Evans, whose wife and daughter financed his legal defense by appearing at the National Theater in San Francisco in a melodrama based on his exploits. It played to packed houses, and one critic wrote after opening night, "The dramatic taste of San Francisco at this time is perhaps not the highest, but this is strong meat."

The decline of train robbery began with the new century. In 1902 it became a federal crime, and in July of 1908 the U.S. Attorney General established the Bureau of Investigation (later the FBI)—modeled, incidentally, on the Pinkerton agency. Improvements were developed in communications, transportation (in 1923 an airplane was used to pursue train robbers for the first time), and forensic science. At the same time the major Western gold and silver strikes were beginning to play out, and precious metal consignments declined. Postal money orders were introduced in the 1880s, travelers' checks in the '90s, and wire transfers in the early part of this century.

The last Western train robbery was a failure and a farce. Harry Loftus was a Chicagoan with a child's fascination with the storybook West and outlaw exploits, and may have been mildly retarded. A Canadian friend, Henry Donaldson, shared his fantasy, and in 1937 they left Chicago for El Paso. There the two duded up in the most outlandish Western gear they could find—checked shirts, rawhide vests, Stetsons big as Chinese gongs, and six-guns—and rode out of town on two bony nags.

In Deming, New Mexico, they sold the horses and holed

up to recover from saddle sores while they planned a daring train robbery. A few days later they boarded the Southern Pacific's westbound Apache Limited, still dressed in all their gunslinger finery.

An hour out of Deming, near Mimbres, Harry Loftus rose from his seat and drew down on the conductor, W. M. Holloway. Holloway was more worried than frightened, because he could see Loftus was nervous and knew nothing about handling a revolver.

While Loftus covered Holloway, Henry Donaldson went down the coach's aisle collecting wallets and watches from the passengers. But when Donaldson reached the last seat, he was jumped by a burly off-duty switchman named W. L. Smith. Loftus, racing to his pard's aid, was tripped by a foot. Men passengers piled on both outlaws, and when Donaldson's gun went off, fatally injuring switchman Smith, the passengers became enraged. Loftus and Donaldson were nearly beaten to death.

It was an ignominious end, and as historian Richard Patterson writes, it "had been too long in coming. It should have ended with Cassidy and Longabaugh [Butch and Sundance]. . . . By 1937 it deserved no better than Henry and Harry."

The first Western movie with a story line was *The Great Train Robbery* (1903, directed by Edwin S. Porter). Although it was shot on a section of Delaware and Lackawanna track near Dover, New Jersey, it is a remarkably polished and authentic film depicting a classic water-stop heist by mounted masked men. *Butch Cassidy and the Sundance Kid* (1969, George Roy Hill) dramatizes several of the Wild Bunch's train jobs, including the one near Wilcox, Wyoming; its literate William Goldman script is quite historically accurate. A minor item of interest is *Love Me Tender* (1956, Robert D. Webb), the first Elvis Presley film. Before Presley was cast, the project was entitled *The Reno Brothers*; the film is a highly romanticized depiction of the brothers' pre-outlaw Civil War days.

The best book-length treatment of the subject is *Train Robbery: The Birth, Flowering, and Decline of a Notorious Western Enterprise*, by Richard Patterson. Besides giving anecdotal accounts of the best-known train jobs, and a few of the more obscure, Patterson places train robbery in a historical and social perspective. *Western Train Robberies*, by Don DeNevi, is mistitled; it is exclusively concerned with California robberies of the Southern Pacific. *Great Train Robberies of the West*, by Eugene B. Block, relates the circumstances of a dozen and a half of the better-known train jobs between 1866 and 1933. Block consistently reports myth as fact, and too often substitutes invention for research.

James D. Horan's Western histories are always meticulously researched, include many rare photographs, and quote extensively from primary sources. Two volumes germane to the present topic are *The Authentic Wild West: The Outlaws*, which includes biographies of the Reno, James, Younger, and Dalton gangs, the Wild Bunch, and Sam Bass. *The Pinkertons: The Detective Dynasty That Made History*, covers in detail the agency's role in apprehending train robbers.

Biographies exist of most of the better-known outlaws, and several—including John Reno, Cole Younger, and Bill Miner—wrote autobiographies. A noteworthy curiosity is *When the Daltons Rode*, by Emmett Dalton, published in 1931. In 1940, three years after Emmett's death, it was made into an excellent if revisionist B-movie of the same title, directed by George Marshall. A Universal Studios publicity photo from that year shows the actors who played the four Dalton boys—Andy Devine, Frank Albertson, Broderick Crawford, and Brian Donlevy—posing with a sad-faced Julia Dalton, Emmett's widow.

William Kittredge
Steven M. Krauzer
Missoula, Montana
Fall, 1982

About the Author

Owen Rountree is the pseudonym of Steven M. Krauzer and William Kittredge, who live in Missoula, Montana. Kittredge has published over forty short stories and is a Professor of English at the University of Montana. Krauzer is a full-time writer who has published five novels in addition to the Cord series. Under their own names, Kittredge and Krauzer have co-edited four anthologies of popular American fiction.

Ride into the world of adventure with Ballantine's western novels!